# CELTIC TALES

# CELTIC TALES

ETHEL MARY WILMOT-BUXTON

**Disclaimer**

Throughout the text, readers may find that some of the language used in dialogue, descriptions or the expressions of opinions is unacceptable by today's standards. These reflect the attitudes and usage common at the time the book was written. In no way do they reflect the attitude of the publishers.

This edition published in 2026 by Arcturus Publishing Limited
26/27 Bickels Yard, 151–153 Bermondsey Street,
London SE1 3HA



AD013028UK
Supplier 40, Date 0226, PI00012897

Printed in the UK

Authorised Representative:
Easy Access System Europe - Mustamäe tee 50, 10621 Tallinn, Estonia
gpsr.requests@easproject.com

# CONTENTS


Introduction .... 7

I THE CHILDREN OF LIR .... 11

II THE QUEST OF THE SEVEN CHAMPIONS .... 15

I. The Seven Champions of Arthur .... 16

II. How the Seven Champions found Olwen of the White Footprints .... 20

III. The Impossible Tasks set by Thornogre Thistlehair .... 25

IV. Two of the Impossible Tasks are Fulfilled .... 29

V. How Prince Kilhugh Won His Bride .... 35

III THE LADY OF THE FOUNTAIN .... 43

I. The Tale of Kynon .... 44

II. The Tale of Owain .... 49

III The Further Adventures of Owain .... 53

IV THE STORY OF KING LUD .... 61

V THE TALE OF TALIESIN .... 67

VI OLGER THE DANE .... 75

I. How Olger became Champion of France .... 76

II. The Vengeance of Olger .... 85

III. The Return from Avalon .... 91

VII THE STORY OF KING FORTAGER .... 99

VIII WILD WALES .... 109

IX THE FASTNESS OF LLEWELYN .... 115

X IN GLENDOWER LAND .... 121

XI A WELSH MARKET-TOWN 127
XII A VISIT TO ANGLESEY AND HOLYHEAD 133
XIII AN EISTEDDFOD 139
XIV "MEN OF HARLECH" 143
XV THE SACRED RIVER 151
XVI A PEEP AT PEMBROKE 155
XVII THE DEVIL'S BRIDGE 163
XVIII THE GLOWING MOUNTAIN 171

# INTRODUCTION

A fellow of the Royal Historical Society, Ethel Mary Wilmot-Buxton (1870-1923) had a deep love of the past and the stories we tell ourselves about ourselves. This book begins with her retelling of old Welsh myths that originally appeared as *Old Celtic Tales* in 1909. Her retellings come from a very English perspective and include ideas about nationalism and religion that should be seen in the context of her time.

Ethel Mary used her initials in her author name, perhaps to ensure that gender prejudice wouldn't affect the reception of her work. In her time, the retelling of folktales and myths in print was dominated by men such as Joseph Jacobs and Andrew Lang. E.M Wilmot-Buxton's biography was such that she would have been immersed in the works of such authors.

She studied at Hughes Hall, Cambridge and, later, taught at Brighton High School for Girls. She was also a translator and wrote numerous books that made the stories of Britain and Europe accessible to school children as well as adults. She was well-known for adapting impenetrable medieval texts into readable, moralised tales for young people.

That morality was pointedly linked to her race, religion, nationality and ideas about other cultures. It might make her prose jarring to the modern reader, but her stories are nevertheless engaging and a fascinating peep into another time. She used the word 'peep' for her series of travelogues and the one included here after the stories from *Old Celtic Tales* is *Peeps at Many Lands: Wales*.

To understand the provenance of the tales Wilmot-Buxton retells, it is useful to look first at *The Mabinogion*, the single most important medieval Welsh source for Celtic narrative in English. *The Mabinogion* is not one book written at a single historical moment but rather an anthology of prose

tales preserved in Welsh manuscripts – most famously the 14th-century *Red Book of Hergest* – that weave myth, heroic adventure, and courtly romance into episodic cycles. The collection includes material variously concerned with gods and otherworldly figures, warrior-heroes, enchantment and transformation, and the social rituals of early Welsh nobility. Its tales are rich in symbolic logic (sibling rivalry, sworn hospitality, magical metamorphosis) and they supply some of the most evocative images associated with Celtic literature (the enchanted island, the shapeshifted animal, the warrior who keeps a fatal promise).

Closely related in the public imagination are the Arthurian legends, the sprawling corpus of stories known as *The Matter of Britain*. Arthurian material ranges from possible early folk memory of a Dark Ages leader through the elaborate medieval romances of Geoffrey of Monmouth, Chrétien de Troyes, and Sir Thomas Malory, among others. The legends migrated and expanded across Europe: courtly love and chivalric quest motifs were grafted onto older British and Welsh material, producing new narrative forms such as the Grail quest and the courtly triangle of Arthur, Guinevere, and Lancelot. Because of this accretionary history, the Arthurian cycle often overlaps with Celtic motifs (islands, prophetic visions, enchanted women), and many retellers, Wilmot-Buxton included, draw from both streams when shaping their versions.

The enduring value of Wilmot-Buxton's *Old Celtic Tales* lies in its invitation: it is a book that asks readers to listen to stories that have shaped British and Irish imaginative life for centuries. Read it as you would a map to a landscape that is partly remembered and partly dreamed, and allow its scenes of sorcery, sorrow and stubborn heroism to reacquaint you with a narrative tradition that continues to resurface in poetry, drama and popular culture.

A good contrast and companion to the tales is Wilmot-Buxton's impressions of Wales. Here landscape and legend meld to create a compelling account of the country. In her descriptive writing she lingers over the geography of the country with its steep green valleys, sudden crags, quiet villages, and winding rivers. She sought out places where history and myth seemed to overlap: ruined castles that once guarded contested borders, abbeys where monks preserved chronicles, and lonely hillsides associated with saints, poets or early princely courts. Her encounters with these settings are painted with an eye for atmosphere: the shifting light on a mountainside, the persistent wind along the coast, the hush that settles over a chapel village on a Sunday morning. Wales, for her, was a land whose physical character made its ancient stories feel not remote but vividly present.

Her visits also brought her into contact with Welsh customs, music, and everyday life, all of which she treated with a blend of affection and curiosity. She describes conversations with local people, market-days bustling beneath looming hills, and small towns that seemed at once ordinary and steeped in antiquity. The sound of choral singing struck her as one of the clearest expressions of the Welsh spirit. These cultural experiences helped shape her understanding of the emotional tone of the Celtic tradition: its emphasis on loyalty, sorrow, bravery, music, and the poignancy of fate. To Wilmot-Buxton, the people she met were not merely modern inhabitants of an old land but inheritors of a long imaginative lineage.

All of this profoundly influenced her retellings of Celtic tales. When she later wrote versions drawn from *The Mabinogion* and Arthurian tradition, her sense of Wales as a place where story and landscape were inseparable gave her narratives a grounded vividness. She had walked through the valleys where legends claimed heroes once roamed, looked

out over lakes tied to enchantments, and traced the outlines of hillforts and ruined courts that echoed the tales. As a result, her adaptations are coloured not only by literary sources but by lived experience: she imbues her stories with the mood of the Welsh countryside, the dignity of its people, and the lingering presence of its mythic past. In this way, her travels did not merely inform her understanding of Celtic material; they gave her the imaginative soil from which her retellings could grow.

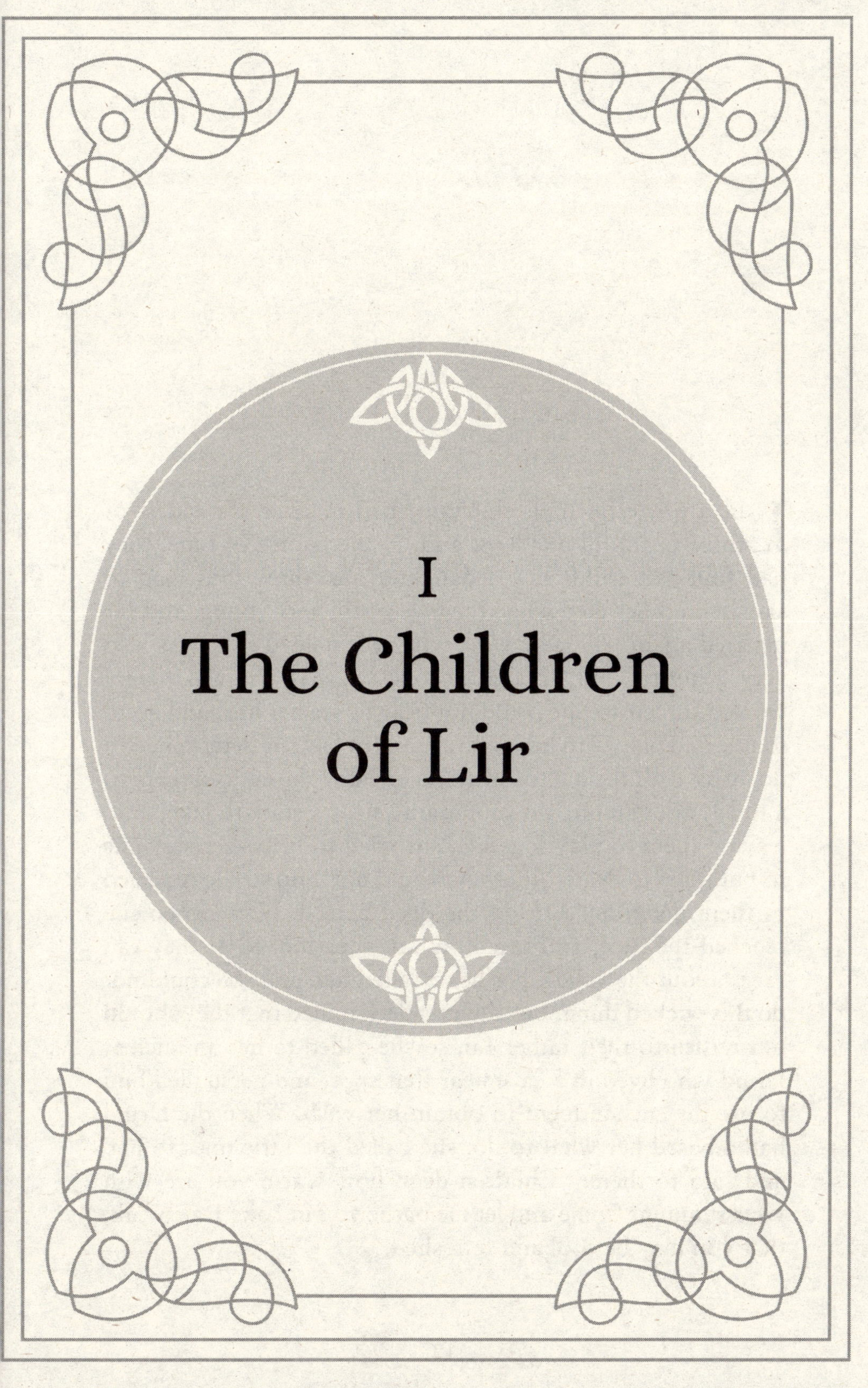

# I
# The Children of Lir

Lir, a powerful Irish chieftain, had married the eldest of three beautiful maidens, and, in the course of time, they had four fair children – a daughter and three sons. Sad to say, the mother died when they were still very young; and Lir married again. His new wife, who was named Eva, was also very beautiful, but, though no one knew it, she was a very wicked sorceress. She could not bear to see her husband go to fondle and play with his children, and at last she determined to do away with them altogether. So one day she enticed them to a lonely spot among the mountains, near a smooth lake, and, leaving them to play together, she tried to bribe her servants to put them to death. But they would not, and so she returned to them determined to do the deed herself. Now, when she reached the spot, and saw how fair they looked as they ran races about the valley, her heart failed her, and she could not do this wicked thing. But she was determined that they should not return to their father Lir, so she called to her an ancient Druid who lived in a cave near that spot, and persuaded him to use his enchantment to obtain her wish. When the Druid had advised her what to do, she called the little ones to her, and said to them: "Children dear, how warm you are with your running! Come and let me bathe you in Lake Dairbreak, that you may be cool and refreshed."

The children were delighted to do so, and were soon splashing about in the clear water, but no sooner had the water covered them than by the magic spells of Eva and the Druid they were all four changed into swans. "Birds shall ye be," chanted the Druid from the bank as the change took place, "until, long ages hence, ye hear the voice of a Christian bell." So the four beautiful milk-white swans swam sadly away over the smooth water; and when the cruel Eva saw what she had done, she feared to face her husband, and repented bitterly of her evil deed. But it was too late. All she could do was to grant to the birds the use of their native speech, their human reason, and the power of singing plaintive fairy music, so sweet that those who heard it should be soothed and calmed, however sad and angry they had been before.

A terrible punishment overtook their wicked persecutor. When the King of that country heard of her cruel deed, he sent for her, and asked: "What shape of all others on the earth, or below the earth, or over the earth, do you most abhor?" She replied: "A demon of the air." Then the King pronounced judgment on her: "A demon of the air shalt thou be till the end of time."

Meantime hundreds of years passed away, and still the beautiful swans swam up and down their lake and looked for deliverance. Sometimes they took flight, and entered the Western Sea, and sailed around the coast; but all Ireland was in heathen darkness, and never the sound of a Christian bell was heard. The dwellers of those coast lands used to visit the shore in crowds to hear their sweet music and watch their graceful movements. But after a time they were caught by the strong current of Mull, and this drove the fair birds into the stormy seas between Erin and Alba. Here they endured many a woe; for sometimes they were separated from one another by the storm and darkness, and sometimes they were almost

frozen to death in the icy floods. And so, tormented by the restless waves and the chill winds of winter, they waited for three hundred years. But one soft spring morning, when the ice-floes had drifted away and the wind sang gently over the mountains, as they floated along their own Lake Dairbreak, they heard the sound of a Christian bell. For St Patrick had come to Ireland with the glad Gospel news, and everywhere men were building churches, and hastening to fill them with worshippers.

So when the sound of the distant bell floated over the water, the spell was broken, and the Children of Lir returned to their own shapes. But they had lived so long that, after they had learnt the Christian faith, they were glad to lie down and rest for ever. They were all buried in the self-same tomb, and after their death men made songs about them; and every Irish boy and girl to this day loves to hear the story of the Swan-Children of Lir.

*From the earliest mythological cycle of Celtic poems. No copy of it is found in writing till the early seventeenth century.*

# II
# The Quest of the Seven Champions

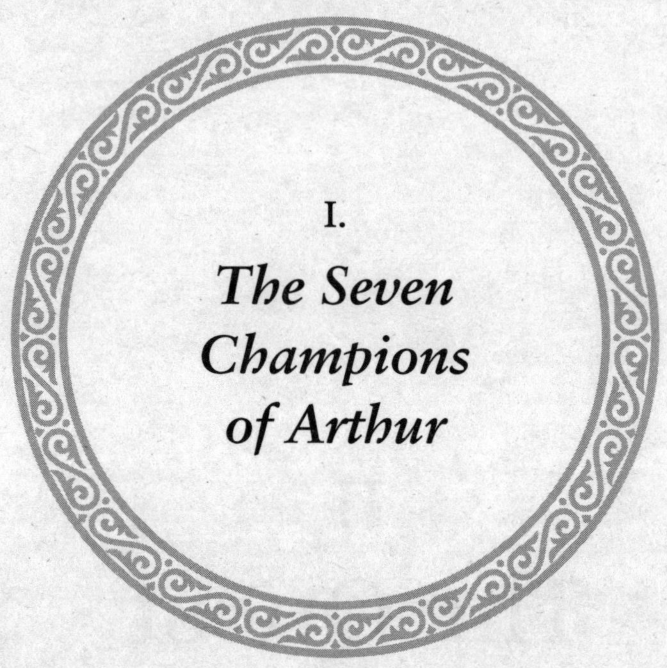

# I.
# *The Seven Champions of Arthur*

These stories were told in old days to British boys and girls as they sat round the fireside and heard the wind outside skirling among the wild Welsh hills. But, no doubt, in time they crossed the border, and were told also to English children, who knew and loved the charming tales of Arthur and his knights.

In the days of King Arthur there lived a noble young prince named Kilhugh, to whom it had been foretold that he should never marry until he could win for his wife the maiden Olwen, daughter of Thornogre Thistlehair, the Chief of the Giants. But, though he was full of love towards the very name of the unknown maid, he could not find out where she lived, nor could anyone tell him anything about her.

He was not cast down, however, but set off upon his steed of dappled grey to seek help from his kinsman Arthur. A fine sight he was, indeed, as he rode along on his prancing horse.

His bridle was made of golden chains, his saddle-cloth of fine purple, from the corners of which hung four golden apples of great value.

His slung war horn was of ivory, his sword of gold, inlaid with a cross that shone like the lightning of heaven; his stirrups also were of pure gold. Two spears with silver shafts were in his hand, and two beautiful greyhounds, wearing collars set with rubies, sprang before him "like two sea-swallows sporting." So lightly did his charger step that the blades of grass did not bend beneath his tread.

At length he came to Arthur's castle, and having with much difficulty satisfied the Chief of the Porters of the Gate, a sturdy warrior known as the Dusky Hero with the Mighty Grasp, he made his way into Arthur's presence, and told the King his story.

"This one boon I crave of thee, O King," he ended, "that thou wilt obtain for me Olwen, the daughter of Thornogre Thistlehair, Chief of the Giants, to be my bride. I ask it of thee and of all thy valiant knights, for the sake of all the fair ladies who have ever lived in this land."

Then Arthur said: "My Prince, I have never heard of this maiden, nor of her kindred, but messengers shall at once set forth to seek her if thou wilt give them time."

So it was agreed that, this being New Year's Day, they should be given until the last day of the year for their quest.

The messengers of Arthur set forth in haste, each taking a different way. They travelled throughout all the land of Britain, the "Island of the Mighty," and then to foreign lands, asking as they went: "Dost thou know aught of Olwen, the daughter of Thornogre Thistlehair, Chief of the Giants?" But everyone said "No."

At length came the end of the year, and on the appointed day the messengers appeared in the wide White Hall of Arthur's

castle, and all alike declared that they had no news whatever to declare concerning the maiden Olwen.

Then Kilhugh was very angry, and said in hasty words: "I alone am denied by my lord the gift I ask. I will depart from hence at once, and take with me the honour of Arthur, whom men call the most honourable King." But Kai, one of the knights, reproved him for his angry speech, and offered to go forth with him and any others who would accompany them, saying: "We will not part till we have found the maiden, or till thou art forced to own she is not among those who dwell on this earth."

So Arthur chose six of his knights to go forth with Prince Kilhugh upon his quest.

First came Kai, whose offer had but just been spoken. An excellent spy and sentinel was he, for he could make himself as tall as the tallest tree in the forest, and so scan all the country round. He could hide himself under water, and lie hidden in lake or river for nine days and nights if need be. Such fire was in his nature that when they needed warmth his companions had but to kindle the piled wood at his finger; he could walk through torrents of rain as dry as on a summer's day; he could go for nine days and nights without sleep, and no doctor could heal the wound made by his sword.

Next came Sir Bedivere, close brother-in-arms to Kai, the swiftest runner, save Arthur himself and one other, in all the land. One-handed was he, yet he could give more wounds in battle than any three warriors together.

Then followed Uriel, who understood the speech of all men and all beasts; and Gawain, who was called the "Hawk of May," because he never returned from any undertaking until it had been performed by him.

The fifth to answer Arthur's call was Merlin, a master of magic, who knew how to put a spell upon the knights that would render them invisible.

Last came Peregrine the Guide, who knew how to find the way as well in a strange country as in his own.

"Go forth, O Chieftains," said the King, "and follow the Prince upon this quest; and great shall be the fame of your adventure."

So the Seven Champions rode forth through the great gates of the palace, and set out with high hearts to seek for Olwen, daughter of Thornogre Thistlehair, Chief of the Giants.

## II.

# *How the Seven Champions found Olwen of the White Footprints*

Onward and onward rode Kilhugh and the six knights until they came at length to a vast plain, stretching in every direction farther than the eye could reach. Over it they rode, and at length perceived through the misty air the towers and battlements of a great castle far away on the borders of the moorland. They rode towards this castle all day long, but yet they never seemed to get any nearer. All the next day they went on riding, and still the castle seemed as far away as ever. The third evening brought them no nearer. At length Sir Gawain exclaimed: "This must be Fleeting Castle, which can always be seen from a distance, but can never be actually reached." Now, on the fourth day, to their surprise, the castle no longer advanced before them as they approached, and soon they were able to draw rein before it, and to wonder in amazement at the thousands of sheep which fed upon the plains surrounding its massive walls. Nearby sat the shepherd

with his dog, tending this enormous flock. The shepherd was a giant in size, and was dressed in the skins of wild beasts. The dog was larger than a full-grown horse; he had the shaggiest of coats, and, though an excellent sheep-dog, was destructive enough elsewhere, for with his fiery breath he would burn up all the dry bushes and dead trees in that region.

The Champions looked somewhat doubtfully at this great animal, and Kai suggested to Uriel that as he knew all tongues, he had better go and speak to the shepherd. "Not I," answered Uriel. "I agreed when we set out to go just as far as thou, and no farther." But Merlin came to them, and explained that he had cast a spell over the dog, so that he could not hurt them. So Kilhugh and Kai and Uriel went together to the shepherd, and asked him very politely who owned that countless flock of sheep, and who lived in yonder castle. "Where have ye lived not to know that?" cried the shepherd. "Everyone in the world ought to know that this is the Castle of Thornogre Thistlehair, Chief of the Giants." "And who art thou?" they asked. "I am Constantine, the brother of Thornogre Thistlehair," replied the man, with an angry look. "A fine brother indeed has he been to me! He has taken from me all my lands and possessions, and now I am obliged to earn a living by feeding his sheep." Then he asked them why they came, and when they replied that they were seeking for Olwen, daughter of Thornogre Thistlehair, he sadly shook his head. "Alas!" he said, "no one ever tried to find her and returned from this place alive. Go back at once, lest ye all perish also." "That will we never do!" cried Kilhugh; and the Champions echoed his words.

Then Constantine inquired who Kilhugh was and, when he heard, he cried out that he was his own nephew, and begged that he and his comrades would spend a night at his house, and to this they readily agreed. And as a mark of affection

Kilhugh gave his uncle a golden ring; but it was much too small for the giant, who put it forthwith into the finger of one of the gloves which hung from his belt as a sign of his rank as chieftain. Then he signalled to his dog, who immediately began to drive the sheep towards home. When they reached the house the giant entered first, and gave his wife his gloves to hold. She soon pulled out the ring, and at once began to question him about it; so he told her that their nephew Kilhugh, with six comrades, was even then dismounting at the door. Then the shepherd's wife was glad, and ran forth with hands outstretched to clasp him in her arms; but so big and strong was she that, as Kai quickly saw, no knight could survive her embrace. So as she threw her arms round Kilhugh's neck, he snatched up a log of firewood, and pushed it into her arms instead of the young prince; and when she unloosed it, it was twisted out of all shape. It was somewhat to their relief, therefore, when she took them into the house without further embracing, and set them down to supper. This was a very frugal meal, and served with great simplicity, for Thornogre had not left his brother so much as a silver goblet or a single chair in his barren hall.

When they had supped, the shepherd's wife asked Kai and Uriel to stay behind after the rest had gone out to the courtyard, and, taking them to the chimney-corner, she opened a great stone box. As she lifted the lid, to their amazement a beautiful boy with golden, curly hair rose up from within. "Pity indeed," exclaimed Uriel, "to keep so handsome a child shut up here. What hath he done?" Then the lady wept, and answered: "All my three and twenty sons have been killed by Thornogre Thistlehair, Chief of the Giants; and now my only hope of keeping him alive is to hide him in this chest, where he has lived ever since he was born." And she wept to think that her boy would never have a chance of doing valiant

deeds and of becoming a great knight. Then Kai bade her be of good cheer and let the lad come with them, promising that he should not be slain unless he, Kai, were killed as well. She agreed to this very gladly, and asked them why they had come to that region. But when she knew they had come to seek for Olwen, she advised them strongly to go home, since in that very quest all her three and twenty sons had perished. They laughed at her fears, however, and asked if the maiden ever came to the shepherd's house. "Yes," said the shepherd's wife; "she comes every Saturday to wash her hair. She leaves behind her all her jewels and rings in the water which she uses, and never asks for them again." Then they begged her to ask fair Olwen to visit her at once, and she agreed, on condition that they would not carry her off against her will. To this the Champions agreed, and sat waiting in a hall for the coming of the maiden.

Very fair she looked as she approached, dressed in a robe of flame-coloured silk, and wearing a jewelled collar of gold round her neck. More yellow was her hair than the flower of the broom, and her skin was whiter than the foam of the wave; and fairer were her hands and fingers than the blossoms of the wood-anemone amidst the spray of the meadow fountain. The eye of the trained hawk, the glance of the falcon were not brighter than hers. Her bosom was more snowy than the breast of the white swan; her cheek was redder than the reddest roses. Whoso beheld her was filled with love of her. Four white trefoils sprang up wherever she trod; therefore was she called Olwen of the White Footprints.

Having entered the house she sat down by Kilhugh, who at once loved her greatly, and began to pray her to come away with him, and be his wife. But Olwen, though she returned his affection, answered that she had promised her father not to go away without his leave. She also told him that Thornogre

knew that her bridal day was fated to be the day of his death, so that he would withhold his leave as long as possible. She advised him, however, to go to her father, and to grant him everything he demanded, and so in time he should win her hand; but if he denied the giant's least request, he would lose both her and his own life. When she had said this, she returned to the castle.

III.

# *The Impossible Tasks set by Thornogre Thistlehair*

The Seven Champions now determined to make their way to the castle, and force an entrance to the hall of Thornogre Thistlehair, Chief of the Giants. It was very dark when they set out, but they easily found their way by the trail of white trefoils which the footprints of Olwen had left. The castle was guarded by nine warders at the gate and nine watch-dogs along the road which led up to it; but a strange silence had fallen upon both men and beasts, and the Champions slew them all without a sound being heard. Then they passed through the great door, and entered the hall of the castle.

Just opposite the entrance sat Thornogre Thistlehair upon a high, wide throne. He was terrible to look upon. His eyebrows were so long and bushy that they fell over his eyes like a curtain, and he was taller and broader than three other giants put together. Close by his hand lay three poisoned darts. After they had greeted him courteously, he asked who

they were; and they replied that they were come from Arthur's Court to ask that Olwen, his daughter, should marry Kilhugh the Prince. Then the giant roared for his pages to come and prop up his eyebrows, that he might see what sort of son-in-law was proposed for him. So when they had propped up his eyebrows he looked angrily at Kilhugh, and bade him come the next day for his answer. But as they went out of the hall, the giant threw one of his poisoned darts at them. Sir Bedivere caught it just in time and threw it back so neatly that it caught the giant in the knee. Then they laughed, and withdrew, leaving him to storm at them, declaring that the great wound hurt him as much as the sting of a gadfly, and that he might never be able to walk quite so well again.

At dawn the next day they returned to the castle, and again demanded the hand of fair Olwen in marriage. But the giant replied: "I can do naught in this matter till I have consulted her four great-grandmothers and her four great-grandfathers. Come again for my answer." So they turned to leave the hall; but as they went the giant snatched up the second of his poisoned darts, and flung it after them. Merlin caught it deftly, however, and threw it back with such force that it entered his chest, and stuck out through his back. This left him grumbling that never again would he be able to climb a hill without losing breath, and fearing lest he now might sometimes suffer from pains in the chest.

The third time they visited the giant he was on his guard, and shouted to them not to dare throw any more darts on pain of death. Then he roared to his pages to lift up his eyebrows, and when they had done it, he snatched up the third poisoned dart, and flung it at them without more ado. But Kilhugh caught it this time, and cast it back at him, so that it pierced one of his eyes. Then, while he grumbled that now his sight would not be so good as before, they went out to dine.

These events made the giant treat his visitors on their next arrival with more civility; besides, he had no more poisoned darts. He once more inquired why they had come, and when he realised that Kilhugh was determined to marry Olwen, he made him promise that he would do all that he required of him in return for his agreement to the marriage. Kilhugh, mindful of Olwen's warning that he was to agree to perform whatever her father proposed, gave a ready promise, and bade him ask away. Then did Thornogre Thistlehair propound to him forty Impossible Things, of which these seven are the chief: Firstly, he must gather nine bushels of flax sown hundreds of years ago in a field of red earth, of which never a seed had sprouted. Not one grain of the measure must be missing, and they must be sown again in a freshly ploughed field to make flax for Olwen's wedding veil. Secondly, he must find Mabon, the son of Modron, who was stolen from his mother when three days old, and had not since been heard of. Thirdly, he must find the Cauldron of Cruseward the Cauldron-Keeper, in which, if one tries to cook food for a coward, one may wait for ever for the water to boil, but if for a brave man the meal is ready directly it is placed therein. In this cauldron must all the food for the wedding feast be prepared. Fourthly, since the giant must shave for the wedding, he must obtain for a razor the tusk of the Boar-headed Branch-breaker, which to be of any use must be taken from his skull while he yet lived. Fifthly, since the giant must wash his hair, all matted together as it was, for the wedding, he must bring to him the Charmed Balsam kept by the Jet-Black Sorceress, daughter of the Snow-White Sorceress, from the Source of the Brook of Sorrow, at the edge of the Twilight Land. Sixthly, that the giant's hair might be smoothed and combed he must bring the scissors and the comb that are found between the ears of Burstingboar, the Wide-Waster, since they alone would

perform the operation without breaking. Seventhly, he must obtain the sword of Garnard the Giant, since that alone would kill the Wide-Waster, from whom, unless he were killed, the comb and scissors could never be obtained.

When he had made an end of speaking, the giant jeered at the Prince, who, unless he could do all these Impossible Things, might never wed his daughter. But Kilhugh answered with a high heart: "I have knights for my companions, horses and hounds, and Arthur is my kinsman. I shall do all that thou requirest, thou wicked giant, and shall win thy daughter, but thou shalt lose thy life."

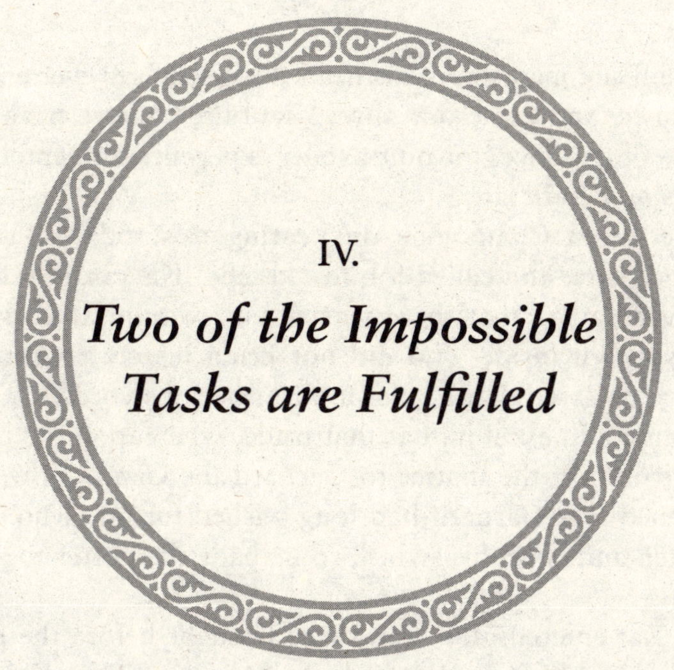

IV.

# *Two of the Impossible Tasks are Fulfilled*

Scarcely had the Seven Champions left the castle of Thornogre Thistlehair when they were joined by the fair-haired son of the shepherd, who had lived all his life in the chest. Eager to make a great name for himself he implored them to let him accompany them, which accordingly they did. Then they turned their faces towards Arthur's castle.

At evening-time they reached the gates of a very great castle, the largest in the world, and as they pulled up their horses before it, an enormous black giant came out of the gate, and looked at them very hard. They greeted him politely, and asked whose castle this was.

"'Tis the castle of Garnard the Giant," he answered.

They looked at each other with glee, for one of the appointed tasks was to obtain the sword of this very giant. Then they asked if he were used to treat strangers courteously.

The black man shook his head. "No stranger ever entered that castle and came out alive," said he; "but ye have little chance of entrance, for no traveller is permitted to enter who knows no handicraft."

The Seven Champions on hearing this rode on to the entrance gate, and called for admittance. The porter refused, however, saying that there was revelry within, and that no man set foot inside who did not bring his craft with him. But Kai declared that he was a burnisher of swords, and that no man could excel him at that trade, whereupon the porter went to report the matter to Garnard the Giant. Now, it so happened that Garnard had long wished for one who could brighten and clean his sword, so he bade the porter to admit him.

So Kai entered alone, and was brought before the giant, who ordered his sword to be brought to him. Then Kai drew out his whetstone, and, first asking if he required it to glitter with a blue or a white lustre, he polished half the blade, and returned it to the giant, saying: "How is that?"

The giant was highly pleased. "If the rest of my sword can be made to look like that," said he, "I shall value it above all my treasures. But how comes it that so clever a craftsman is wandering about alone without a companion?"

"But I have a companion," said Kai, "a cunning craftsman, too, though not at this work. Send, I pray you, and admit him. And the porter shall know him by this sign: the head of his lance shall spring into the air, draw blood from the wind, and return to its place again."

Then the porter opened the gate, and Bedivere marched into the hall, ready for what might befall, and stood watching Kai as he went on polishing the sword. This being done, to gain more time he asked for the sheath, and he fell to mending it and putting in new sides of wood.

Meantime, as he had hoped, while all the porters and followers of the giant stood gaping round him, the young son of the herdsman had managed to climb over the castle wall, and to help his companions over also, whereupon they were able to make their way to hiding-places behind doors and pillars, from which they could see the company in the hall without being seen themselves.

By this time Kai had finished both sword and scabbard, and, stepping up to the giant's great chair, pretended to hand them to him. But, as the giant was off his guard, he lifted the sword, and brought it down on Garnard's neck, so that he cut off his head. Before his followers could lay hands on Kai and Bedivere, the knights rushed out upon them, and slew them all. Then, having loaded themselves with gold and jewels, but above all with the precious sword, they set forth again for Arthur's palace.

This time they reached it in safety, and, having told their story, asked the advice of the King as to which of the six remaining quests they should first undertake. To seek out Mabon, the son of Modron, was Arthur's decision; and for this undertaking he chose Uriel because he could understand the speech of both animals and birds, as well as that of all strange men; and Idwel, because he was Mabon's kinsman, with Kai and Bedivere, because they were known never to turn back from any adventure until it was accomplished.

So these four set out upon their quest.

Now, Mabon had been lost so long ago that not the oldest man on the earth, nor their great-grandfathers before them, had ever heard anything at all about him. But Idwel remembered that many birds and beasts live much longer than the oldest man, so they determined to seek out the oldest of these.

"And who," said they, "could be older than the Ousel of Deepdell? Let us seek her help."

So they made their way through a great forest till they came to a shadowy place, where on a small stone sat the Ousel of Deepdell; and her they implored to tell them if she knew anything of Mabon, son of Modron, who was taken from between his mother and the wall when he was only three days old.

"When I first came here," answered the Ousel gravely, "I was but a fledgling. On this spot where I now sit stood a smith's stone anvil. Since then no hand has touched it, but every evening I have pecked at it with my beak as I smoothed my feathers before sleeping. Now all that remains of it is this little pebble upon which I sit. Yet through all the years that have passed while this change took place I have never heard of Mabon, the son of Modron. But do not despair: I will take you to a race of creatures who were made before me, and them ye shall inquire of again."

Then she took them to a place where, at the foot of an ancient oak, lay the Stag of the Fern Brake. Of him they once more asked the question: "Dost thou know anything of Mabon, son of Modron, parted from his mother when three days old?"

The Stag answered: "When first I came here this great forest was a vast plain, in which grew one little oak sapling. This sapling became in time an oak-tree, and after its long lifetime gradually decayed until it became this stump. Now, an oak-tree is three hundred years in growing, three hundred years in its full strength, and three hundred years in its decay. Yet in all this time I have never heard aught of Mabon, son of Modron. But, since ye are Arthur's knights, I will take you to one who was made before my time." Then he led them to the Owl of Darkdingle.

"When first I came here," said the Owl from his dark cavernous home when he heard their question, "this valley

was covered with a vast wood. It decayed away, and another grew up, and after that had withered away, a third, which now ye see. But never have I heard of the man whom ye seek. Yet, since ye are Arthur's knights, I will take ye to the oldest creature in the world—to the Eagle of the Aldergrove."

So thither they went, and when he heard their question the Eagle answered: "When I first arrived, there was a rock in this place so high that I could perch on its top and peck at the stars, and so long have I been here that now it is but a few inches high. Never have I heard of this man save once, and that was when I visited the Lone Lake. There I stuck my claws into a salmon, hoping to kill him for my supper; but he dragged me into deep water, so that I barely escaped with my life. But when I went with all my band to slay him, he sent ambassadors, and made good peace with me, and came and begged me to take fifty fish-spears out of his back. He, if anyone can, will tell you what you want to know, and I will be your guide to him."

So they journeyed on till they reached a great blue lake, hidden in the depths of the forest, and there they found the Salmon of the Lone Lake. He heard their question and, looking at them very wisely, replied: "Such wrong as I have never found elsewhere have I found under the walls of Gloucester Castle, on the River Severn, up which I travel with every tide. And that ye may know it is so, come, two of ye, and travel thither upon my shoulders."

Then Kai and Uriel came down to the water, and stood upon the shoulders of the Salmon of Lone Lake, who swam with them down the Severn, and brought them under the walls of Gloucester Castle.

"Hark!" said the Salmon; and as they listened, a voice was heard from the dungeon wall wailing in deepest sorrow and woe. Then Uriel cried: "Whose voice is this that moans within this gloomy cell?"

"Alas!" wailed the voice, "'tis that of Mabon, the son of Modron, shut up eternally in the prison of Gwyn, son of Nith, King of Faerie. Here I, the Elfin Huntsman, ever young, am shut out eternally from the sight of wood and fell and the joyful chase which is my birthright."

"Canst thou be ransomed with silver and gold?" asked Uriel.

"No," answered Mabon; "if ever I am rescued from this cruel place it must be by battle and strife."

Then Uriel and Kai returned to their companions.

Seeing that this was the kind of adventure that Arthur loved, they journeyed back to the King, and told him all. So he prepared a great army, and marched by land to attack Gloucester Castle. But while he fought before the gates, Kai and Bedivere had sailed down the river on the shoulders of the Salmon of Lone Lake, and, finding the water-side portion of the Castle unprotected, they broke through the wall, and carried off Mabon, the son of Modron, and he returned with them to Arthur's Court.

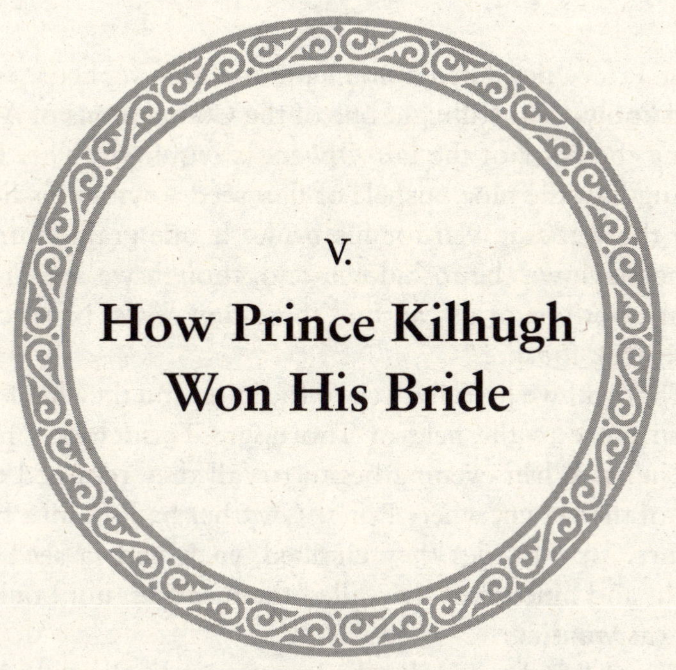

V.

# How Prince Kilhugh Won His Bride

While Arthur and his knights were discussing which of the Impossible Tasks should next be undertaken, it so happened that a certain prince, named Gwyther, who was also one of Arthur's knights, was walking over a mountain in his own country, the Land of the Dawn. And as he walked, deep in thought, he heard a sad little cry. Up and down he looked, but nothing could he see that could explain such mournful cry. But presently it came again from under his very feet, and there he saw an ant-hill. Inside the ant-hill the little creatures were wailing piteously, for the heath on the mountain-side was afire, and in a short time their kingdom would be all in a blaze.

Then Prince Gwyther drew his sword, and cut off the ant-hill at a blow, and threw it into a place of safety.

"Our grateful thanks are thine," cried the ants. "Now tell us what we can do for thee in return, Prince Gwyther of the Land of the Dawn."

The Prince pondered a moment, and then replied: "All the world knows that Kilhugh, one of the Companions of Arthur, seeking the hand of the fair Olwen, is required by her father to bring him the nine bushels of flax seed sown in his field to make the wedding veil for his bride. If one grain is missing the marriage will be forbidden; and, though we are Arthur's knights, not one of us can find these tiny seeds. Now, can ye do this task for me?"

"That will we joyfully," cried the ants, and they made their way in haste to the field of Thornogre Thistlehair, Chief of the Giants. When evening began to fall they returned to the Land of the Dawn, where Prince Gwyther had set up a bushel measure. Up its sides they climbed, each with a seed in its mouth; and nine times they filled the measure, until only one seed was wanting.

"'Tis well," they cried; "the lame emmet has not yet come home." And before nightfall the lame emmet toiled up to the bushel measure, and dropped in the last seed.

So the nine bushels of flax seed were taken to the castle of Arthur, and given to Prince Kilhugh.

Then said King Arthur: "Let us now go to Ireland to seek for the Cauldron of Cruseward the Steward of Odgar, the Irish King." Now, this cauldron, as you will remember, was of such a kind that when food for a coward was cooked in it the food remained as it was at first, but if for a brave man it was ready for eating directly it was placed in the pot. So it was very precious; and when Arthur's request for it was received by Odgar, Cruseward replied in wrath: "Not a glimpse of my cauldron shall he obtain, even if it would give him all the blessings in the world; much less will I give it him altogether."

Then Arthur called together his men of war, and sailed over the stormy seas to Ireland. When the people saw him in battle array, they were afraid, and counselled Odgar to

receive him peaceably. So Odgar sent friendly messages, and invited him to a banquet in his palace. Now when the banquet was over, Odgar was about to give presents to his guests, but Arthur would take nothing. He wanted naught, he said, but the Cauldron of Cruseward. When Cruseward heard this, he thundered out: "Nay, King Arthur, I will never give it to thee. If thou couldst have it for the asking it would have been given at the bidding of King Odgar, not at thine."

When Bedivere heard this rude reply he was very angry, and, rushing upon him, seized the cauldron, and set it on the shoulders of Arthur's Cauldron-Bearer. Then swords were drawn, and the men of Arthur's host fell upon Cruseward and his followers, and slew them. Thus they carried off the cauldron, and bore it, full of Irish gold, back to the Island of the Mighty.

After this adventure they set forth to obtain the Charmed Balsam that was guarded by the Jet-Black Sorceress, daughter of the Snow-White Sorceress, at the Brook of Sorrow, on the edge of the Twilight Land. And when they approached the dismal cavern where she dwelt, King Arthur was joined by Gwyn of the Twilight Land, and Gwyther from the Land of the Dawn, who, knowing the Sorceress and her power, advised that two of his attendants should first be sent into the cave. Directly the first appeared the Sorceress seized him by the hair, and threw him down, and trampled on him. The second dragged her away from him, but could do nothing against her, for she kicked them and beat them and thrust them forth again.

Then Arthur would have gone in himself; but Prince Gwyn and Prince Gwyther prevented him, saying it would not be a fitting adventure for so great a king, and persuaded him to send in the two Tall Brothers. But these two were so ill treated by the Sorceress that they came out more dead than alive, and had

to be lifted on to their horses. Then, when he saw his followers so ill used, nothing could keep Arthur back. He rushed into the cave, and with one stroke of his dagger, killed the wicked Sorceress, while Kai carried off the Charmed Balsam.

They next set out to hunt the Boar-headed Branch-breaker; but soon they heard that no man could pluck out the tusk from the living head of this terrible animal but Odgar, King of Ireland. With some difficulty they persuaded him to accompany them; but at length the huntsmen gathered together, with him at their head, and a great hunt for the boar began. The swiftest dogs could not bring the animal to bay, until at length Arthur's own hound, Cavall, brought him to the ground, and Odgar rushed up to pull out the tusk; but he would have been killed, had not Kai been there to strike the Branch-breaker down directly Odgar had plucked it out.

There yet remained to seek out the jewelled scissors and comb that were between the ears of Burstingboar, the Wide-Waster. Now, this Burstingboar had laid waste a great part of Ireland, so that all men went in terror of him; and, that the heroes might not be misled about the curious things said to lie between his ears, Merlin was sent to Ireland to seek him out and see if it were as the giant had said.

So Merlin tracked Burstingboar to his den on Cold Blast Ridge, and, having changed himself into a bird, flew down into a thicket close by. From thence he could see the creature lying on the ground, with his seven young boars at his side, and between his ears twinkled the jewels of the scissors and the comb. Then Merlin thought it was a sad thing that the heroes should lose their lives for such things, and determined to try to carry them off himself. So he flew upon the head of Burstingboar, and tried to snatch up the razor; but all he really got was a great bristle. Then Burstingboar rose up in a great rage, foaming at the mouth. He could see no one; but a

fleck of the poisonous foam fell upon Merlin, and hurt him so that he never quite recovered.

When he heard this news, Arthur gathered together such a number of brave knights and squires that the Irish feared he was about to attack their land, but when he told them he had come to deliver them from the dreaded Burstingboar, their joy knew no bounds. And so it was arranged that those Irish who had joined his host should first attack the boar; then, if he still lived, he should be attacked by Arthur's own knights; and if by that time he were not slain, Arthur should himself hunt him on the third day.

But the first day and the second saw the boar triumphant; and when Arthur took his turn he fought for nine days and nights without even wounding the creature or one of his cubs. At the end of that time all the knights besought Arthur to tell them the secret about the boar, which all this time he had kept.

Then Arthur told them that the creature had once been a king, but for his sins and his great pride had been changed into a boar. And he sent Uriel to confer with him concerning the jewelled comb and scissors. But when Uriel spoke gently to him, bidding him deliver these up at the request of Arthur, the boar grew very fierce, and said: "Not only shall Arthur never even see these jewels, but I with my young ones will go forthwith and harry the land of Arthur, doing all the hurt to it that we can."

When they heard this news all the host arose at dawn to prevent them leaving Ireland; but when they looked towards the sea, there was the boar with his young ones swimming far away to the coast of Britain. And before the King could cross the Irish Sea, the boars had landed at Milford Haven, and destroyed every living thing in the neighbourhood.

Then terror fell on all the land, and eagerly men looked for Arthur to come to their aid, who, when he arrived, set out

at once with a crowd of mighty huntsmen to kill the beasts. But it was exceeding hard to find the boar, though his tracks were well marked by the ruin of flocks and men; and when they did come up with him, he slew with his mighty tusks a full half-dozen of Arthur's followers, and dashed off to a mountain-top, where they lost all sign of him: neither man nor dog could tell whither he had disappeared.

At last they heard that the boars were ravaging a valley some miles away. Thither they followed and, after a hard struggle, they killed the young boars one by one. But after a long pursuit Burstingboar vanished again, so completely this time that the host returned to Cornwall, thinking he must have left the land.

Scarcely had Arthur entered his palace when a breathless messenger rushed into the hall. "Arise!" he cried. "The boar is ruining thy domain, trampling down towers and towns, uprooting trees, and killing men and cattle on all sides, and he is now coming over the mountains to do the same in Cornwall."

Then Arthur made this speech to his followers: "Men of the Island of the Mighty, Burstingboar, the Wide-Waster, has slain many of our bravest men, but he shall never enter Cornwall while I live. You may do as you please; but for me, I will no longer hunt him, but shall meet him face to face."

Forthwith he posted men at various spots to prevent the creature from landing, and then rode up to the river's brink. As he arrived, suddenly, with a great rush, Burstingboar sprang out of the forest, and tried to cross on his way to Cornwall. But Arthur and his companions drove their horses into the water, and followed him, and somehow or other seized him by his fore feet as he scrambled up the bank, and flung him back into the river; and as he fell, Mabon, the son of Modron, caught the razor from behind one of his ears, and Kenneder the Wild snatched the scissors from behind the other.

Yet, even while they did this, Burstingboar upreared himself from the water, dashed up the river-bank, and disappeared. Then all the host followed, but they only came up to him when he had got well into Cornwall. Then a desperate fight began. By harassing him all day they managed to keep him from ravaging the land, and when he tried to get into Devon they were too many for him. Over the moors, down the coombs, up the hills, they chased him, till at length, being desperate, he turned, and made for the sea. In he plunged, but, though the pursuing horses stayed their feet at the water's edge, those two good hounds, Raceapace and Boundoft, who had followed him so long, could not hold themselves back, but plunged in after him into the waves. For long the heroes watched his course, with those two fierce dogs close behind him; but from that day to this nothing more has ever been heard of either Burstingboar or the two hounds.

Now, all the Impossible Tasks had been fulfilled, and joyfully did Prince Kilhugh ride to the giant's castle to claim his bride. But Thornogre Thistlehair looked on in gloomy silence as the marvels were spread out before him; he allowed himself to be shaven and combed; but though he could not refuse to give the Prince his daughter's hand, he openly said that he did it with no good will. Then the herdsman's son stood forth, and cried: "O giant, three and twenty of my brothers thou hast foully slain, and defrauded my father of his heritage. For these things thou shalt surely die by my hand to-day." So he dragged him by his hair to the castle battlements, and, being very strong, he slew him there, and cut off his head. And the castle was given to the herdsman; but Kilhugh married fair Olwen, and they were happy ever after as long as they both lived.

*From the "Mabinogion," A Welsh Romance. Thirteenth century A.D.*

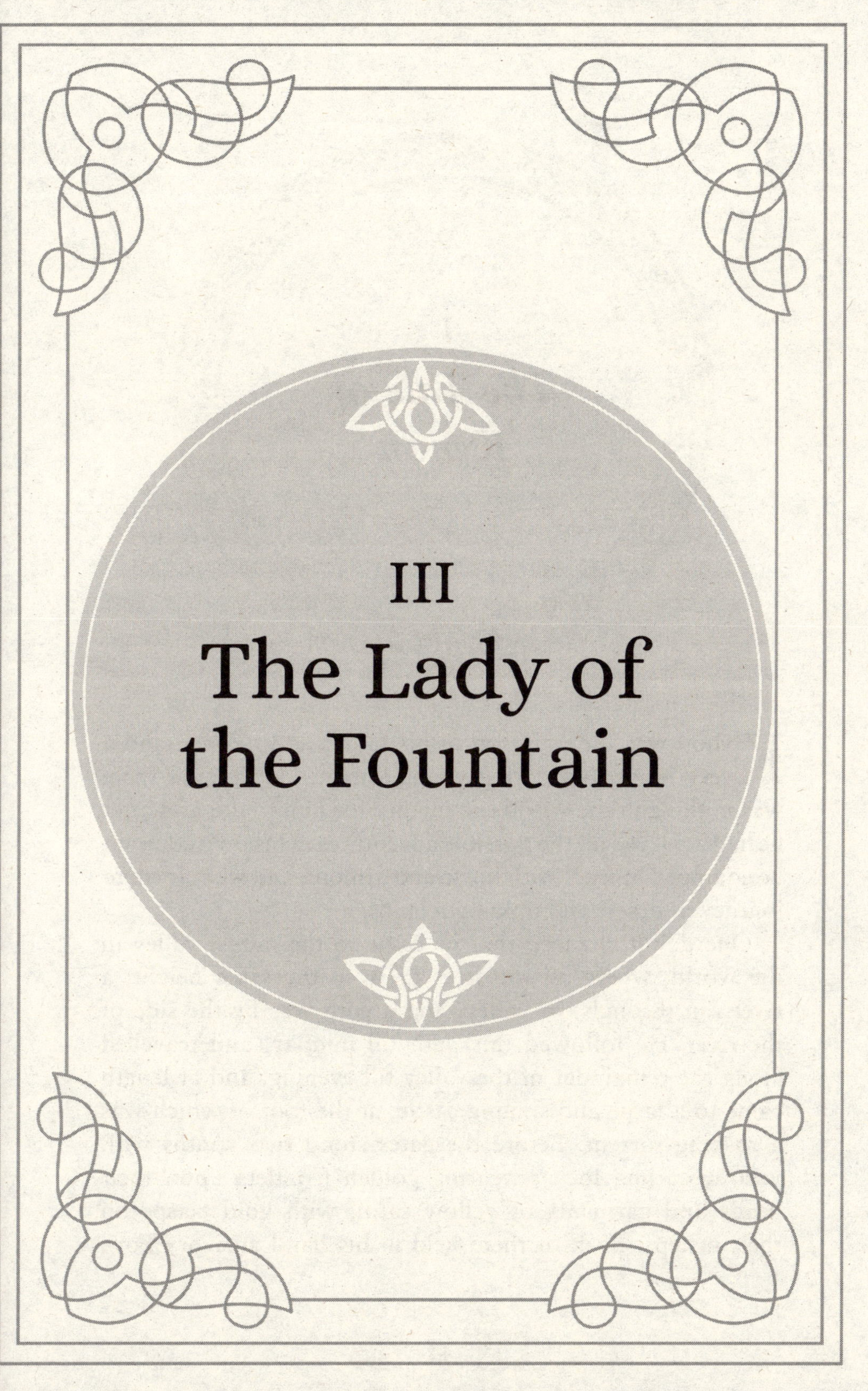

# III
# The Lady of the Fountain

# I.
# *The Tale of Kynon*

Kynon was the only son of his father and mother, and a very brave and daring young knight. He thought there was nothing in the world too mighty for him to do; and after he had achieved all the possible adventures in his own country, he equipped himself with horse and armour, and went forth to journey in desert and unknown lands.

One day it chanced that he came to the fairest valley in the world, where all the trees grew to the same height; a river ran through the valley, and a path was by the side of the river. He followed this path till midday, and travelled along the remainder of the valley till evening, and at length came to a large and shining castle, at the foot of which was a rushing torrent. Before the gates stood two youths with yellow, curling locks, wearing golden frontlets upon their heads and garments of yellow satin, with gold clasps on their insteps. Each of them held in his hand an ivory bow,

and their arrows were winged with peacock's feathers. Their daggers had blades of gold and hilts of whalebone, and they played with them as they stood, shooting them to and fro. They allowed Kynon to pass into the courtyard, and there he saw a man, in the prime of life, also clad in a robe of yellow satin, and round the top of his yellow mantle was a band of gold lace. He received Kynon with great courtesy, and at once conducted him into the hall of the castle. In the hall sat four and twenty damsels embroidering satin at a window, and they were all so very fair that the eyes of Kynon were almost dazzled at the sight of so much beauty. They rose at his coming, and six of them took his horse, and unbuckled his armour; six more took his weapons, and washed them in a basin till they shone like the sun; another six spread cloths on the table and prepared meat; and the last six took off his soiled cloak and doublet, and put on garments of fine linen and yellow satin, with a broad gold band round the mantle. Then they gave him cushions of red linen on which to sit, and brought bowls of silver full of water wherein to wash, and towels, some of green linen, some of white. Presently, when all was ready, they sat down to eat at a silver table, with cloths of the finest linen, and the meats that were brought were of the most delicious flavour in the world.

At length, when the stranger's hunger was appeased, the Man in Yellow began to inquire who he was, and what was the cause of his journey. And Kynon told him that he was trying to find out if anyone were his superior, or whether he could gain the mastery over all. The Man in Yellow smiled, saying: "If I did not fear that harm would come to thee I would show thee that thou seekest."

Then Kynon implored him to make trial of him, and at length the man agreed. "Sleep here to-night," said he, "and on the morning arise early, and take the road upward through

the valley till you come to the wood by which you came. A little way within the wood you will find a path branching off to the right. Follow this until you come to a large, sheltered glade, with a mound in the centre. On the top of the mound you will see a black man of great size, larger than two men of this world. He has but one foot, and one eye in the middle of his forehead. In his hand he holds a club which no two men could lift. He is exceedingly ill-favoured to look at, and he is the warden of that wood. And round about him you will see grazing a thousand wild animals. Inquire of him the way out of the glade, and he will point out the road which will lead you to that of which you are in quest."

Next morning Kynon arose very early, and rode away. All came to pass as the Man in Yellow had said, except that the black man was of huger size and his club looked far heavier than Kynon had been led to suppose. When Kynon saw the thousand animals browsing around the mound and the black man sitting on the top of it, he asked what power he held over those creatures.

"I will show thee, little man," said he; and, taking up his club, he struck one of the stags a great blow. The stag brayed loudly, and at the sound all the animals came together, as many as the stars in the sky, so that Kynon scarcely found room to stand. Serpents were there, and dragons, and every kind of beast. Then the black man looked at them, and bade them go feed; and they all bowed their heads, and did homage to him ere they departed.

Then Kynon asked the way out of the glade; and when the man knew his reason he said to him: "Take the path that leads towards the head of the glade, and ascend the woody steeps until you reach the summit; there you will find an open space like a large valley, and in the midst of it a tall tree, with branches greener than the greenest pine-trees.

"Beneath this tree is a fountain, and by the fountain a marble slab, and on the slab a silver bowl attached by a silver chain. Take the bowl, and throw a bowlful of water on the slab, and you shall see what will happen. And if you do not find trouble in that adventure you need not seek it during the rest of your life."

So Kynon did as he had said, and found the fountain, and threw a bowlful of water upon the slab. And immediately there came a mighty peal of thunder, so that the earth shook. With the thunder came a shower of hailstones, so heavy that each one pierced to the bone, and Kynon could only endure it by placing his shield over his own and his horse's head. After that the weather became fair; but when he looked at the tree—behold!—there was not a single leaf left upon it. Then a flock of birds came, and alighted on the tree, and never was heard such sweet strains as those they sang; and while he was listening to the birds a murmuring voice rose through the valley, like a gust of wind, which said: "O knight, what has brought you hither? What evil have I done to you that you should act towards me and my possessions as you have this day? Do you not know that the shower to-day has left alive neither beast nor man that was exposed to it?"

Scarcely had the voice died away when there appeared a knight clad in black velvet, riding a coal-black horse, who made a rush at Kynon then and there. And the onset was so furious, and Kynon so little prepared, that he was overthrown. Then the Black Knight passed the shaft of his lance through the bridle-rein of Kynon's horse, and, without a glance at his fallen adversary, rode off the way he had come. There was nothing left for the fallen knight but to make his way back to the castle. The black man jeered aloud at him as he passed through the glade, and, with much anger and mortification, the knight hurried on to the castle of the Man in Yellow.

There he was received with the utmost hospitality; and no one alluded to his adventure, nor did he mention it to any. On the next day he found, ready saddled, a dark bay horse, with nostrils as red as scarlet, and, mounted on this, he returned to Arthur's Court.

# II.
# *The Tale of Owain*

When Kynon had related at Arthur's Court the story of his adventure with the Black Knight, one of his companions, Owain by name, said: "Is it not befitting that one of us go and discover this place?"

"It is very well to talk about it," said Sir Kai, "but 'tis harder to carry it out."

Then Owain went away, and prepared his horse and his armour, and very early next morning he rode away in the direction which Kynon had pointed out to him.

In due time he reached the castle, and was kindly received by the Man in Yellow, and set down before a very excellent meal. And the four and twenty maidens seemed even lovelier to Owain than they had to Kynon.

When they asked him his errand Owain replied that he was in quest of the knight who guards the fountain; and the Yellow Man, though very reluctantly, pointed out the way. All

happened to Owain as it had to Kynon, save that the shower seemed more violent and the song of the birds even sweeter than before. And as they sang the Black Knight appeared, and rode violently upon Owain; but he was prepared to receive him, and they fought fiercely together. Their lances broke with the shock of their attack, and, drawing their swords, they fought until Owain struck the knight a blow which pierced through helmet, skull, and brain.

Then the Black Knight, knowing he had received a mortal blow, turned his horse, and fled. But Owain pursued hard after him until they came to a lordly castle. When they reached the gate the Black Knight was allowed to enter; but Owain was so close behind that, when the portcullis fell, it struck his horse behind the saddle, and cut him in two, carrying away the rowels of the spurs which were on Owain's heels. So the rowels and part of the horse were outside and Owain was shut up inside with the other part of the horse between the two gates, for the inner one was closed.

As the knight stood wondering what would happen next he saw through an opening in the upper part of the gate a street facing him, with a row of houses on either side; and from one of these houses came out a maiden, with yellow, curling locks, dressed in yellow satin, with shoes of parti-coloured leather. She approached the gate, and desired him to open it.

"Truly, lady," said Owain ruefully, "I can no more open it for you than you can for me."

"That is very sad," said the damsel; "yet it is the part of every woman to do what she can to succour you, for you are a loyal squire of dames, so I will do whatever is in my power for you. Take this ring, and put it on your finger, with the stone inside your hand, and close your hand upon the stone. As long as you conceal it, it will conceal you. Presently, when they have consulted together, they will come to fetch you, in

order to put you to death, and will be much upset when they cannot find you. But I shall sit on the horse-block yonder, and you will see me though I cannot see you. Come, therefore, and put your hand upon my shoulder, that I may know you are near; and whichever way I go, do you follow me."

So Owain vanished from the sight of men, and sorely grieved were his foes when they came to seek him and found only part of his horse. But he found the maiden, and laid his hand upon her shoulder; and she led him to a splendid chamber, where even the nails were painted in beautiful colours, and there she gave him abundance of food in silver dishes, and left him to rest.

Now, on that night the nobleman who owned the castle, whom Owain had so grievously wounded, died; and the maiden of the golden locks presently brought Owain to a window from whence he might see the funeral procession. And foremost among the mourners walked the Countess of that domain. She was so very beautiful that Owain fell deeply in love with her, and said to the maiden: "Verily, there goes the woman I love best in the world."

"Truly," said the maiden, "she too shall love you not a little, and I will go woo for thee."

So the maiden, whose name was Luned, went to the chamber of her mistress the Countess, and found her weeping, because now the Black Knight was slain, there was no one to defend her dominions. For so it was that, so long as the fountain was safe, all was well, but if that were not defended, all her lands would soon be lost.

Then Luned said: "Surely you know that no one can defend the fountain except he be a knight of Arthur's household. Let me go to Arthur's Court, and I will bring back with me a warrior who can guard the fountain as well as, or even better than, he who kept it formerly."

"That will be a hard task," said the Countess. "Go, however, and make good that which thou hast promised."

But Luned did not go to Arthur's Court; she went instead to the chamber of Owain, and, having warned him to wait until it was due time, hid herself as long as it would have taken to travel to the Court.

Then she brought Owain a coat and mantle of yellow satin, on which were bands of broad gold lace; and for his feet shoes of softest leather, fastened by golden clasps in the shape of lions; and thus they proceeded to the chamber of the Countess.

But when they arrived the Countess looked steadfastly upon Owain, and said: "Luned, this knight has not the appearance of a traveller."

"Well, lady, he is none the worse for that," said Luned.

"I am certain," said the Countess, "that this is the man who killed my master, the Black Knight."

"So much the better for you, lady," replied Luned, "for if he had not been stronger than your master, he could not have killed him. There is no use in crying over spilt milk."

Then the Countess looked again on Owain, and when she saw he was a very goodly knight, and courageous withal, she began to return his affection for her; and soon afterwards they were married.

So Owain defended the fountain with lance and sword; and whenever a knight came there, he overthrew him, and ransomed him for his full worth, and what he then obtained he divided among his barons and his knights, so that he became very much beloved. And so three years passed away.

# III
# *The Further Adventures of Owain*

When three long years had gone by, King Arthur began to get very sad because he heard nothing of his good knight Owain. And when the others saw his sadness they suggested that he and the men of his household should go and seek Owain. So they set off; and Kynon was their guide. They spent the night at the castle of the Man in Yellow, and he and his twenty-four damsels waited upon them with the utmost hospitality. In the morning they set off for the wood, and, passing the black man, they came to the fountain. Then Sir Kai begged that he might throw the water on the slab and receive the adventure that first befell. All happened as before, save that several of the attendants were killed by the hail-storm; and as they stood listening to the song of the birds, a knight clad in black satin, riding on a coal-black horse, spurred up to Sir Kai, and in a few minutes Sir Kai was overthrown.

Then the knight rode off, and the host of Arthur encamped as darkness drew on.

The next day Sir Kai met the Black Knight again, and this time was wounded very sorely. Then each of the knights in turn fought, and all were overthrown save one, and he was called Gwalchmai. The fight between him and the Black Knight was very fierce, but at length a heavy blow broke the helmet of Gwalchmai, and showed his face. And, behold, the Black Knight threw down his sword, and embraced him, saying: "Little did I know that you were my cousin Gwalchmai." Then did Gwalchmai know the voice of Owain, and embraced him, and brought him to Arthur, and everyone was glad to see the long-lost knight again.

So all the company proceeded to the castle of the Countess of the Fountain, and there partook of a great banquet, which had been three years preparing; for Owain had always said that Arthur would come to seek him. And when all was over Arthur prepared to depart, but first he sent a message to the Countess, begging her to permit Owain to go and visit him for the space of three months. So Owain departed, though much against the will of his Countess; and when he was once more among his kindred and friends he forgot all about his wife and the People in Yellow, and stayed away three years instead of three months. At the end of these three years, as Owain sat one day at meat in the royal city of Caerleon-on-Usk, there rode through the doorway of the hall a damsel on a bay horse covered with foam, wearing a bridle and saddle of gold; and the damsel was clad in a robe of yellow satin. She came up to Owain, and, taking the ring from off his hand, "Thus," she said, "shall be treated the deceiver, the traitor, the faithless and the disgraced." Then she turned her horse's head, and rode away.

Then was Owain deeply ashamed and sorrowful; and on the next day he left the Court, and wandered to the distant parts

of the country and to waste places and barren mountains. And he stayed there until his clothes were worn out and his body wasted away and his hair grown long. His only companions were the wild beasts with whom he fed, and they grew to love him as their friend; but after a time he became so weak that he could no longer abide with them, so he descended from the mountains into the fairest park in all the world, which was said to belong to a widowed countess.

One day the Countess and her maidens were walking by a lake that was in the middle of the park, when they saw in the pathway the prostrate figure of a man. At first they thought he was dead; but they went near, and touched him, and found there was life in him, though he was very much exhausted. So the Countess returned to the castle, and sent one of her maidens with a flask full of precious balsam to the sick man, together with a horse and a good suit of clothes, and said: "Go with these, and place them near the man we saw just now. Anoint him with the balsam near his heart, and if there is still life in him he will arise through the strength of the balsam. Then watch what he will do."

The maiden departed, and forthwith poured the whole of the balsam on Owain, and left the horse and the garments close by, and hid herself, and watched what would happen. Presently he began to move his hands, then his arms, and then all at once he rose up, and was ashamed to see how ragged and dirty he looked. Then he perceived the horse, and the garments; so he washed in the lake, and crept to the horse, and with difficulty clothed himself, and clambered on to the saddle. Then came the maiden from her hiding-place, and he was rejoiced to see her, and asked her to whom the park belonged.

"Truly," said she, "a widowed countess owns park and castle, which are all that are left to her of two noble earldoms

left to her by her late husband. All the rest has been taken from her by a neighbouring earl because she refused to become his wife."

"That is a pity," said Owain. And the maiden conducted him to the castle, and brought him to a pleasant room, and left him there. Then she went to the Countess, and gave her back the flask. "Ha! damsel," said her mistress, "where is all the balsam?" "Have I not used it all?" said she. "O maiden," said the Countess, "thou hast wasted for me seven-score pounds' worth of ointment on an unknown stranger. However, now that he is here, wait thou upon him until he is quite recovered."

So the maiden tended Owain, and gave him meat and drink and medicine until he was well again. And in three months he was as comely a knight as ever he had been before. One day he heard a great tumult in the castle, and asked the maiden the cause thereof. She told him that the earl whom she had mentioned before had come against the Countess with a large army to force her to marry him. "Has she a horse and arms to spare?" asked Owain. "She has the best in the world," said she.

"Then go and beg the loan of them," said Owain, "that I may go and have a look at this earl." "I will," said the maiden. So she made her request to the Countess; but the lady laughed a bitter laugh, and said: "He may as well have them to-day as my enemy to-morrow; but I know not what he would do with them."

Then they brought out a beautiful black horse, with a beechen saddle, and a suit of armour for man and horse; and Owain armed himself, and rode forth, attended by two pages. When they came in sight of the enemy they could not see where the army ended, it was so great; but Owain asked where the earl himself was and, when he was pointed out,

he sent the pages back to the castle, and rode forward till he met the earl. And Owain was now so strong that he drew the earl completely out of the saddle, and turned his horse's head towards the castle, and, although it was no easy task, brought the earl to the gate. When they had entered, he gave the earl as a gift to the Countess, and said to her: "Lo, here is a return to you for your wondrous balsam."

Then the earl restored to the Countess her two earldoms in ransom for his life, and for his freedom he gave her half his own domains and all his jewels and gold and silver.

After this Owain departed from the castle, though all honoured him greatly and begged him to stay with them. But he was still ashamed and sorrowful at heart, and preferred rather to ride forth into desert places again.

One day, as he was journeying through a wood, he heard a great uproar, and, riding forward, found a great craggy mound, on the side of which was a grey rock. In the rock was a cleft, and in the cleft a serpent; and nearby stood a black lion, and every time the lion moved to go hence the serpent darted towards him to attack him.

Then Owain unsheathed his sword, and struck the serpent, and cut him in two, and went on his way. But, strange to say, the lion followed him, and played about him like a dog. All that day they travelled together; and at night Owain dismounted, and turned his horse loose in a woody meadow. And he kindled a fire, the lion bringing him wood enough to last for three nights. Then the lion disappeared and, after a while, returned bearing a fine, large roebuck, which he laid before Owain; and when it was skinned and roasted, it made an excellent supper for them both. As he was eating, he heard a deep sigh near him, which was repeated three times.

"Who is there?" asked Owain. "A mortal maiden," was the reply. "Who art thou?" he asked again. And the voice replied:

"I am Luned, the handmaiden of the Countess of the Fountain. In this stone vault am I imprisoned on account of the knight who came from Arthur's Court and married my Countess. For a short time only he stayed with her, and then went away, and has never returned—and he was the friend I loved most in the world. And one day two of the pages of the Countess's chamber reviled him, and called him ill names, and I told them that they two were not a match for him alone. Then they imprisoned me in this stone cell, and said I should be put to death unless he came himself to deliver me by a certain day—and that is the day after to-morrow. But I have no one to send to seek him for me. And his name is Owain, the son of Urien."

Then Owain said: "Art thou certain that if the knight knew all this, he would come to your rescue?"

"I am most certain of it," said she.

So Owain bade her hope for the best, and meantime bade her tell him if there were any place near, where he could get lodging for the night. She bade him follow the river, so he rode along till he came to a very fine castle. The Earl who ruled over the place received him very hospitably, and good fodder was given to his horse. But the lion went and lay down in the horse's manger, so that none of the men of the castle dared to approach him. Meantime Owain had been brought in to supper; and very soon the lion came, and sat between his knees, and shared his food. Then Owain noticed that everyone in the castle was very sorrowful. The Earl sat on one side of him, and his fair young daughter on the other; and he never saw anyone look as sad as they.

In the middle of supper the Earl began to bid Owain welcome, adding: "Heaven knows it is not thy coming which makes us sorrowful, but we have good cause for care."

"How is that?" asked Owain.

"I have two sons," replied the Earl, "who went yesterday

to hunt upon the mountains. But on the mountains lives an evil monster who kills men and devours them, and he has seized my sons; and to-morrow he will bring them here, and will devour them before my eyes, unless I will deliver my sweet daughter into his hands. He has the form of a man, but the strength of a giant, and no one can do aught against him."

"Truly this is a hard case," said Owain. "And what wilt thou do?"

"Heaven knows," said the Earl. "But I can never give up my young daughter to be destroyed by him; yet I cannot bear to lose my two brave sons."

So no more was said, and Owain stayed there that night.

Next morning a great noise was heard as the giant entered the courtyard, dragging behind him the two youths by the hair of their heads. Then Owain put on his armour, and went out to fight the giant, and the lion followed him. The giant made a great rush upon the knight; and the lion fought on Owain's side, more fiercely than his master. At length the giant said: "I could easily settle this business with you were it not for the animal that is with you." So Owain shut the lion up inside the castle walls, and went back to fight the giant as before. But the lion heard that it was going ill with Owain; and he roared very loud, and climbed up till he reached the top of the castle, and then sprang down from the walls, and joined his master. And very soon he gave the giant such a stroke with his paw that the monster fell down dead.

Then the Earl was full of gratitude, and begged Owain to remain with him; but he would only stay one more night, and on the morrow set out for the meadow where Luned was imprisoned in the mound. When he reached the spot, he found a great fire kindled, and two youths with curling auburn hair were leading the maiden forth to cast her in the fire.

"Why are you treating her thus?" asked Owain.

They told him of the compact that was between them concerning the maiden. "Owain has failed her," said they, "therefore she must be burnt according to our agreement."

"Well," said Owain, "I know him for a good knight, and if he had known of the maiden's peril he would have come to her rescue; but if you will accept me in his stead I will do battle for her."

This was agreed; and the fight began. But the two were together stronger than Owain, and he was hard beset. Then the lion came to his help, and they two were stronger than the young men. So they said to him: "Chieftain, we did not agree to fight with thy lion, but only with thee." Then Owain shut the lion up in the stone vault where the maiden had been imprisoned, and blocked up the entrance with stones, and returned to the fight. But he was weak from loss of blood, and the young men pressed hard upon him; and the lion roared like thunder when he heard that his master was in trouble, and he burst through the wall, and rushed upon the young men, and slew them both.

So Luned was saved, and glad was she when she found it was Owain indeed who had come to her rescue. Together they sought the dominions of the Countess of the Fountain; and she and Owain and the lion and Luned lived all happily together for the rest of their lives.

*From the "Mabinogion."*

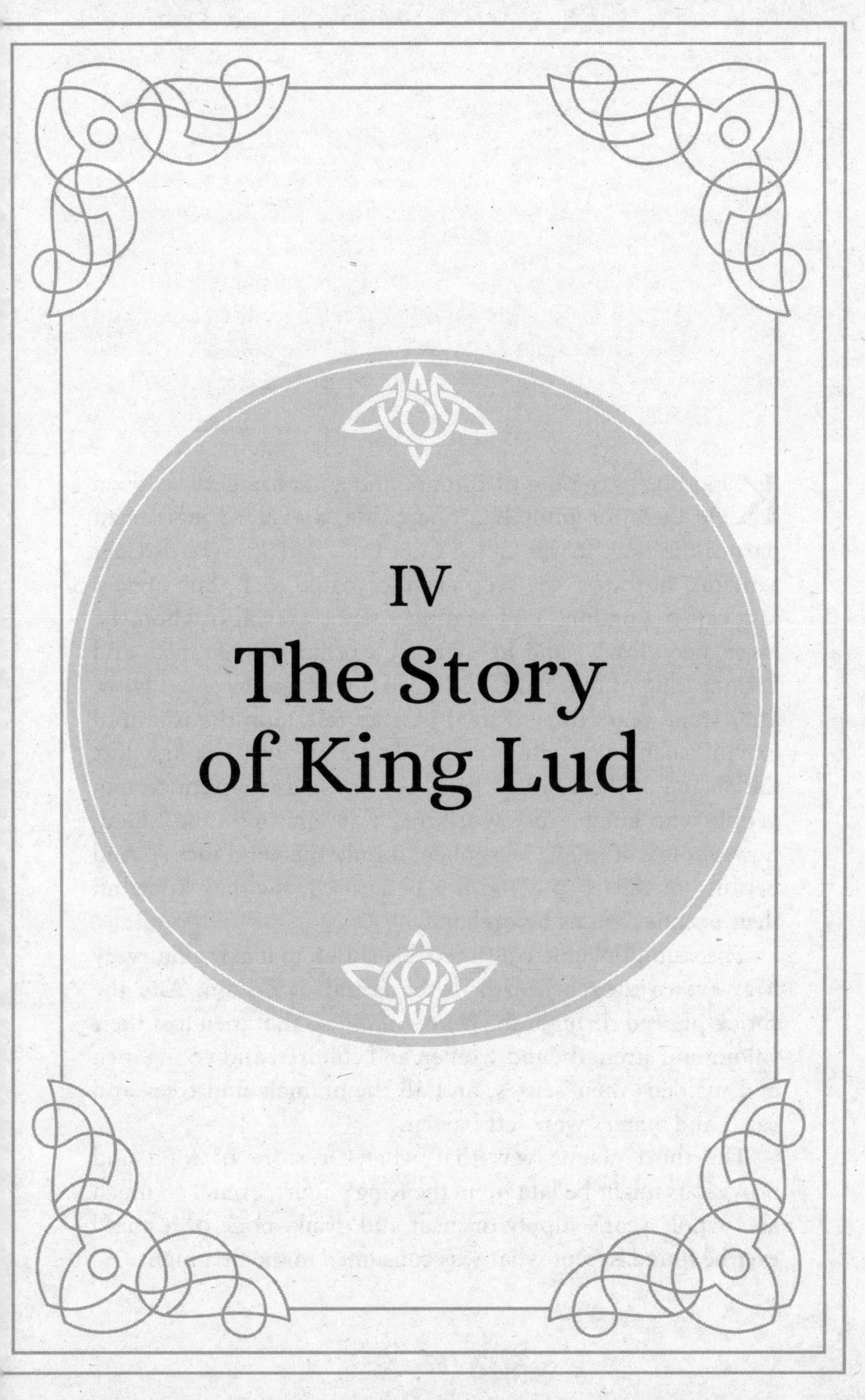

# IV
# The Story of King Lud

King Lud was King of Britain, and a very mighty warrior. He built for himself a fine castle, and lived in it most part of the year. It was called Caer Lud, and afterwards Caer London, but after the stranger race came to Britain it was just called London. Lud had a brother, Llevelys, whom he loved very dearly; and he married a princess of France, and became king of that land, and ruled it well and happily. Now, after some years three dismal plagues fell upon the island of Britain, such as no other land had ever known. The first was the plague of the Coranians. These Coranians were a certain people who knew every word that was said upon the island, however low it might be spoken, if only the wind met it. And because of this they could not be injured, for they knew all their enemies' plans beforehand.

The second plague was a terrible shriek that came on every May-eve over each hearth in the island of Britain. And the shriek pierced through the hearts of all, so that men lost their valour and strength, and women and children and young men and maidens their senses, and all the animals and trees and earth and waters were left barren.

The third plague was that whatever store of food and provisions might be laid up in the King's court, even if so much as a whole year's supply of meat and drink, none of it could ever be found except what was consumed in the first night.

Then King Lud was very sad at heart, because he knew not how to free his land from the dismal plagues. He called together all the nobles of his kingdom, and asked counsel as to what he should do in the midst of these afflictions. And they all advised him to go to France and seek the advice of Llevelys his brother, king of that land. So they made ready a fleet in secrecy and silence, lest the Coranian race should learn the cause of their journey; and Lud, with some of his chosen followers, set his face towards France. When Llevelys saw his brother's ship approaching, he went out to meet him, and embraced him with much joy. Then King Lud told him the purpose of his errand; and King Llevelys thought a while, and, being very wise, soon discovered the cause of those dismal plagues. But they dared not talk freely about them to each other, lest the wind should catch their words, and the Coranians have knowledge of their discourse. So Llevelys caused a long horn to be made of brass, and through this horn they discoursed. But whatever words they spoke into the horn one to the other neither of them could hear anything but harsh and unfriendly words.

Then Llevelys saw that there was a demon in the horn thwarting all their purposes, and caused wine to be put in to wash it out; and through the virtue of the wine the demon was driven away.

When this was done, Llevelys told his brother through the horn that he would give him some insects, which he must take and bruise in water. And when he returned to his kingdom he must call together all the people, both of his own race and the Coranians, as though with the idea of making peace between them. And when they were all together he must take the charmed water made with the bruised insects, and cast it over all alike. And the water would poison the race of the Coranians, but it would not harm those of his own people.

"The second plague," he said, "that of the weird shriek, is caused by a dragon. Another dragon of a foreign race is fighting with it, and striving to overcome it, and for this reason does your dragon make a fearful outcry once every year. This must you do to rid yourself of this plague: cause the island to be measured in its length and breadth, and in the place where you find the exact central point, cause a pit to be dug; and in the pit you must place a cauldron full of the best mead that can be made, with a covering of satin over the face of the cauldron. Then remain there watching, and presently you will see the dragons fighting a terrific fight. Presently they will take the form of dragons of the air; and lastly, when they are worn out with the fury of their fighting, they will fall upon the covering of the cauldron in the form of two pigs, and they will sink in, and the covering with them, till they reach the bottom of the cauldron; and they will drink up all the mead, and after that they will go to sleep. Then you must immediately fold the covering around them, and shut them up in the strongest vessel in your dominions, and hide them deep in the earth. And so long as they shall bide in that strong vessel no plague shall come from elsewhere upon the island of Britain.

"The third plague," continued Llevelys, "is caused by a mighty magician, who takes your meat and drink and stores of provisions. Through his illusions and charms he causes everyone to sleep. Therefore must you watch your food yourself. And, lest he should overcome you with sleep, have a cauldron of ice-cold water by your side, and if you begin to get drowsy, plunge into the cauldron."

Then Lud thanked his brother for his good counsel, and returned to his own land. And first he summoned a meeting of all the people, both of his own race and that of the Coranians; and he bruised the insects in water, and cast it over the heads

of all of them. Immediately it destroyed all the race of the Coranians, but his own people were hurt not at all.

And this was the end of the first dismal plague.

Then he caused the land to be measured in its length and its breadth; and he found the central point in Oxford, and in that place he caused the pit to be dug and the cauldron of mead to be placed, with a covering of satin over the face of it. There he presently beheld the dragons fighting; and when they were weary, they fell into the mead under the shape of pigs, and when they had drunk up all the mead, they slept. And Lud folded the covering round them, and hid them in the strongest place he had on Snowdon. And so the fierce shriek ceased to be heard in his dominions; and this was the end of the second dismal plague.

When this was all ended, King Lud caused a very great banquet to be prepared in the Court. And when it was ready, he placed a cauldron of ice-cold water by his side, and sat down to watch over the banquet. And about the third watch of the night he heard sweet music and gentle songs, which lulled him to sleep. But when he found himself getting very drowsy, he went often into the ice-cold water. At length a man of great size, clad in strong, heavy armour, came in, bearing a hamper; and into this hamper he began to put all the food and provisions of meat and drink, and proceeded to go forth with it. And King Lud was so stupefied with astonishment that one hamper could possibly hold so much, that he had almost let him go. At last, however, he recovered his senses, and rushed after him, and cried: "Stay, stay. Though thou hast done me many insults and stolen much spoil ere now, yet shalt thou do so no more, unless thy skill in arms be better than mine." The magician instantly put down the hamper, and rushed upon him; and they fought so desperately that fire flew from their arms. At length the victory was to Lud, and

he threw the plague to the earth. Then the magician besought him for his life, and promised to serve him as his vassal, and put all his power in the hands of the King, if he would release him; and to this King Lud agreed.

And this was the end of the third dismal plague. From that time forth King Lud reigned in peace and happiness in the island of Britain.

*From the "Mabinogion."*

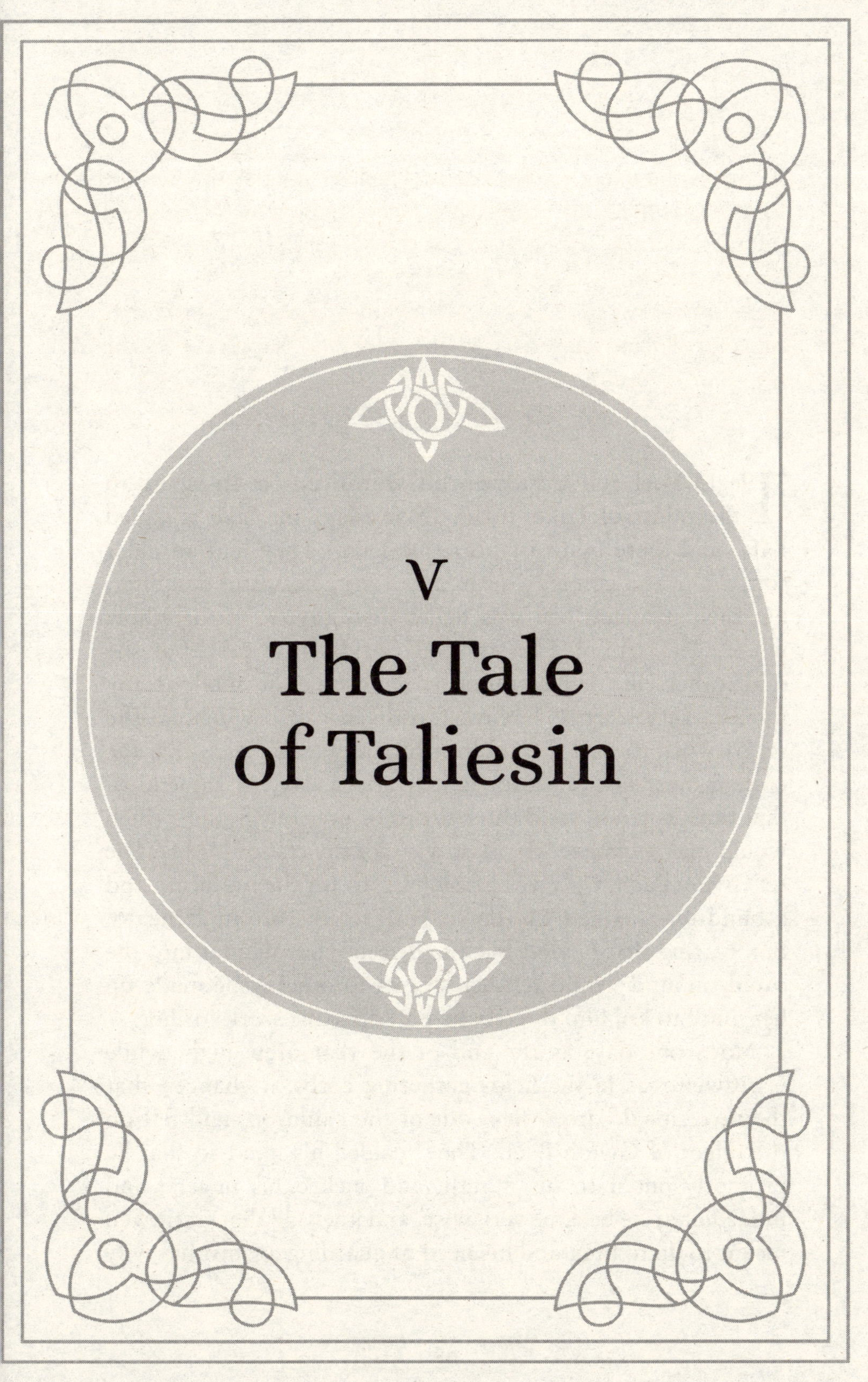

# V
# The Tale of Taliesin

Tegid Voel and Caridwen his wife lived on an island in the midst of Lake Tegid. (Nowadays the lake is called Bala, and there is no island to be seen.) They had an elder son, a fair and comely youth, and a very beautiful daughter; but their youngest son was uglier than anyone in the whole world. This troubled his mother Caridwen at first; but she said to herself: "If he cannot be handsome, he shall, at any rate, be very learned." Now, Caridwen was a witch, so she set to work to boil a Cauldron of Knowledge, of which the boiling must not cease for a year and a day. At the end of that time it would yield three drops of precious liquid, which would make whoever drank it wise for the rest of his life. She set Gwion Bach, who was passing by, to stir the cauldron, and a blind man named Morda to keep up the fire underneath; but, fearing that Gwion Bach had seen what she put into the cauldron, and would tell her secrets to others, she made up her mind to kill him directly he had done his work for her.

Now, one day, as the end of the year drew nigh, while Caridwen was in the fields gathering herbs, it chanced that the three magic drops flew out of the cauldron, and fell on the finger of Gwion Bach. They scalded his hand so that he promptly put it to his mouth, and sucked his fingers; and immediately he became very wise, and knew all that Caridwen meant to do to him, and his need of guarding against her wily

plots! He fled from the house, therefore, and ran towards his own land; and the cauldron, left unstirred, burst in two, and the poisonous liquid ran out of the door, and into a stream where the horses of Gwyddno were drinking; and when they had drunk of the poisoned water they all died.

When Caridwen returned, and saw the year's work was lost, she took up a billet of wood, and began to beat the blind man Morda. But he answered: "You do wrong to beat me; the loss was not because of me."

"You speak truly," said Caridwen. "It was Gwion Bach who robbed me." And she set to running after him as fast as she could. He soon looked back, and saw her, and changed himself into a hare; for the magic liquid had given him many different kinds of skill. But as he fled, she changed herself into a greyhound, and had nearly caught him up when he ran towards a river and changed himself into a fish. Then she became an otter, and chased him till in his weariness he took the form of a bird. But she at once changed herself into a hawk, and gave him no rest in the sky.

Just as he was in fear of death, he saw a heap of grains of wheat on the floor of a barn; so he dropped among them, and became one of the grains. Then Caridwen changed herself into a high-crested black hen, and scratched among the grains till she found him. She was just about to swallow him, when, with his last remaining effort of skill, he became a very beautiful little child, and when she looked at him she had not the heart to kill him on the spot. So she took her own form again, and, having put the child into a leathern bag, she cast him into the sea just below the weir of Gwyddno, which is not far from Aberystwith, on the 29th of April. Then Caridwen returned home again, and thought no more of the matter.

Now, it had been the custom on every May-day eve to go fishing in that weir, and every year fish were taken to the value

of a hundred pounds. Its owner, Gwyddno, had an only son named Elphin, the most unlucky of youths, who was always needing and never getting. This year his father, pitying his ill fortune, granted to him all the weir should contain on May-day, in order to give him something wherewith to begin the world. So the nets were set to catch the fish below the weir, and next day Elphin hurried to see how many they had caught. But the nets were quite empty, and nothing was to be found but a leathern bag which had caught in one of the poles of the weir. Then said one of his companions: "Men were unfortunate before, but never so much as now, when your luck has turned away the fish from a weir that has been worth a hundred pounds every May-eve till now, when there is nothing but a skin in it."

"Perhaps," said Elphin, "the bag may have something in it which is worth a hundred pounds." So his friend hooked up the bag, and opened it, and there peeped out the bright face of a little lad. "See, what a bright face within the bag!" cried his companion. And Elphin said: "Let him be called Taliesin, then" (which means "bright or shining face"), and lifted the child gently on to his horse, and made it walk softly, and went homeward with a very heavy heart.

But as he rode along, the boy behind him sang to him a song of consolation so sweetly that Elphin was much amazed, and asked how he had learnt so beautiful a song. The child replied that, though he was very little, he was notwithstanding very wise.

Then Elphin asked if he were a mortal child or a spirit; upon which the boy sang another song, telling what he had been, and how he had fled from Caridwen, and how he came to be entangled in the weir.

When Elphin reached the house of his father, the latter asked him if his haul were good.

"Father," he answered, "I have caught a poet-minstrel."

"Alas! What good will that do thee?" said Gwyddno.

And Taliesin answered for himself: "He will do him more good than the weir ever did for thee."

Then Gwyddno looked at him, and said: "Art thou able to speak when thou art so little?" And the child replied: "I am better able to speak than thou to question." "What canst thou say?" asked Gwyddno. Upon which Taliesin sang a song of such wondrous beauty, that everyone hastened to the spot to hear the marvellous child.

Soon afterwards Elphin, with his usual ill luck, managed to offend the powerful King Maelgwn, who cast him into a dungeon barred by thirteen locked doors. But when father Gwyddno was lamenting his son's ill fate, the child Taliesin bade him be of good cheer, since he was going to rescue him. Setting off at daybreak he reached the King's palace at the time of the evening meal, and entered the hall just as the bards were beginning to sing the praises of the King, as was their custom every evening. Then Taliesin cast a spell upon these bards, so that instead of singing they could only pout out their lips and make mouths at the King. He forced them also, by his magic power, to tap their fingers on their mouths, as they tried in vain to sing, making a curious sound like "Bler-m! Bler-m!"

The King, naturally, thought they were treating him with great disrespect, and ordered one of his squires to give a blow to the chief bard; and the squire took a broom, and struck him on the head, so that he fell back on his seat. This rough treatment seemed to bring him to his senses, and he then explained that they could not help themselves, but had been put under a spell by a spirit, who was sitting in a corner of the hall under the form of a child. So the King ordered the squire to fetch the child; and Taliesin, nothing loth, was brought up

to the head of the table. Being asked who he was and whence he came, he at once proceeded to sing another wonderful song, in which he informed them that he was the chief bard of Elphin, that his native country was the land of Cherubim, but that at present he was dwelling upon this earth, and might even stay here until the Judgment Day.

The King and his nobles marvelled greatly, for they had never heard the like from a boy so young as he. But as he was the bard of Elphin, who had offended His Majesty, the King determined that his own bards should get the better of him in song. So he ordered the chief bard to stand forth, and then all the four and twenty of them, to strive with Taliesin. But when they came forward to do his bidding they could do no other than play "Bler-m! Bler-m!" on their lips.

Then the King, angry and disappointed, asked the boy Taliesin his errand.

And the child replied in song: "I am come to deliver Elphin, who is imprisoned in this castle, behind thirteen locks."

"I will never let him go," said the King.

Then Taliesin foretold that there should come up from the sea-marshes a wonderful golden worm, which would take revenge upon the King for his cruelty; but, finding his threat had no effect, he turned, and left the hall. Outside the castle he sang a charm to the wind, bidding it blow open the prison of Elphin; and while he thus sang, near the door, there suddenly uprose such a storm of wind that the King and his nobles crouched in terror, expecting that the castle would fall upon their heads. Directly he realised that this was the work of the mysterious child-bard he sent for Elphin from the prison, and implored Taliesin to stay the wind-storm, which he accordingly did. So Elphin was brought into the hall, loaded with chains; at sight of which Taliesin sang another charm song, and the chains immediately fell off his hands and feet. By this time the

King was so full of admiration for the skill and wisdom of the boy that he begged him to take the spell off his own bards, and to test them with questions.

So Taliesin set them free from his charm, and then began to rain questions upon them.

"Why is a stone hard?"

"Why is a thorn sharp-pointed?"

"What is as salt as brine?"

"Who rides the gale?"

"Why is a wheel round?"

"Why is the speech of the tongue different from any other gift?"

These were some of the questions he put, and ended with: "If you and your bards are able, let them give an answer to me, Taliesin."

But none of them could answer a single word.

Then the King dismissed them all with scorn; but still he would not let Elphin go free away.

Then Taliesin bade Elphin wager the King that he had a horse both better and swifter than the King's horses. The King accepted the challenge, and fixed day and time and place for the wager to be tried, and promised him his freedom if he should win the race. The King went thither with all his people and four and twenty of the swiftest horses he possessed. The course was marked out and the horses placed for running. Then came Taliesin with four and twenty twigs of holly, which he had burnt black, and he bade the youth who was to ride his master's horse to place them in his belt. Then he ordered him to let all the King's horses get before him, and, as he should overtake one horse after another, to strike the horse with a holly twig over the crupper, and then let that twig fall, and then to take another twig, and do the same to every one of the horses as he should overtake them.

Moreover, he bade the horseman to watch carefully where his own horse should stumble, and to throw down his cap on the spot. All this was done, and—behold!—each horse that was struck with the holly twig began to lag behind, and the horse of Elphin easily won the race. When all was over, Taliesin brought his master to the spot where his horse had stumbled, and ordered workmen to dig a hole there; and when they had dug deep enough they found a cauldron full of gold. Then said Taliesin: "Elphin, take thou this as a reward for having taken me out of the weir and reared me from that time until now."

So Elphin went home a rich man to his father, and the work of Taliesin was accomplished.

*From the Welsh Romance of Taliesin. Thirteenth century.*

# VI
# Olger the Dane

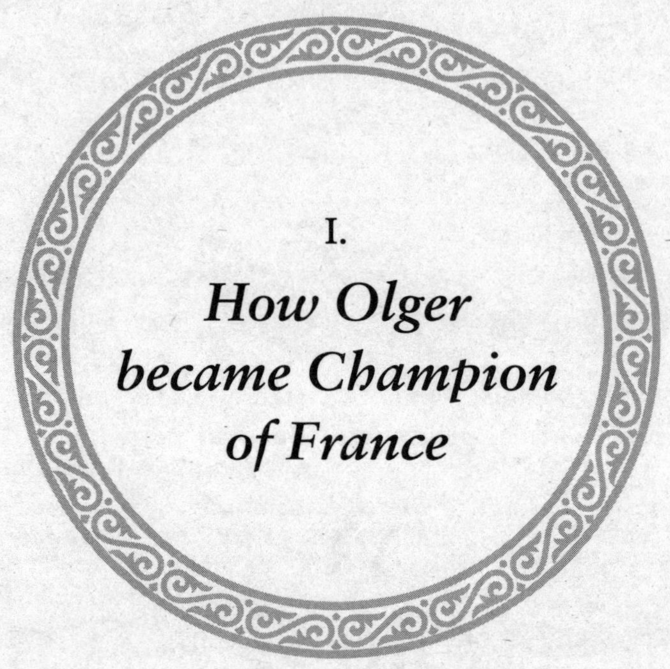

## I.

## *How Olger became Champion of France*

Long ago, in the days when Denmark and England were almost like one country, the palace of the King of the Danes was dark and gloomy, and the sound of weeping and wailing rose within its walls; for the fair young queen, whom all the people loved, had died in giving birth to a son. When she was dead, they took the babe from her arms, and, having called him Olger, they carried him away to the royal nursery, and laid him on a quilted bed of down, and left him there alone. But ere long a sound of rustling was heard in the silent room, and there assembled round the bed six beautiful fairies, who smiled and kissed their hands to him; and the babe smiled back in return.

Then the Fairy Glorian took the child in her arms, and kissed him, and said: "My gift to you is that you shall be the strongest and bravest knight of all your time."

"And mine," said the Fairy Palestine, "is that you shall always have battles to fight."

"No man shall ever conquer you," promised the Fairy Pharamond.

"You shall ever be sweet and gentle," said Meliora.

And Pristina added: "You shall be dear to all women, and happy in your love."

Then Morgan le Fay, who was queen of all the fairies, took the boy in her arms, and pressed his head to her bosom, saying: "Sweet little one, there are few gifts for me to give you; but this shall be mine: You shall never die; and after you have lived a life of glory here you shall be mine, and shall dwell with me for ever in Avalon, the land of Faery." Then she kissed him many times, and laid him back upon the bed; and with soft rustling of wings the fays departed.

Ten years passed away, and Olger had grown a brave, strong boy, and comely to look upon.

At that time it befell that the Emperor Charles the Great sent a message to Godfrey, King of Denmark, and father of young Olger, to bid him come and do homage for his lands; to which King Godfrey, being a stout and stalwart man, made bold answer: "Tell Charles I hold my lands of God and of my good sword; and if he doubt it, let him come and see. Homage to him I will not do." So Charles the Great came up against him with a mighty army, and after long fighting King Godfrey was defeated, and forced to promise to appear before the Emperor every Easter to do allegiance. And, fearing lest he would not keep his word, the Emperor demanded that young Olger should be given to him as a hostage. To this King Godfrey agreed; and the boy was carried off to the Emperor's Court, and there instructed in all the arts and learning of the time, and so grew up an accomplished and handsome youth.

For three years King Godfrey appeared each Easter to do allegiance; but in the meantime he had married again. And

when another son was born to him, his new wife persuaded him to cease to humble himself before the Emperor, for she hoped that by this means Olger would be put to death, and her own son would inherit the kingdom. So on the fourth Easter the King of Denmark appeared not at the Court; and so they took young Olger, and threw him into the prison of the Castle of St Omer, until messengers should find out why King Godfrey had broken his pledged word.

Now, the keeper of the castle was very good to the young man, who also found much favour in the eyes of his wife, and those of Bellisande, his daughter, who loved him from the first moment he appeared.

Instead of a gloomy dungeon Olger was placed in a rich apartment, hung with beautiful tapestry, and Bellisande herself was proud to wait upon him.

Meantime the messengers of Charles had met with a shameful reception at the hands of Godfrey, King of Denmark. Their ears and noses were slit, their heads shaven, and they were driven from the kingdom. Full of shame and wrath they appeared at the Court of their master, and cried loudly for revenge against Godfrey, and against his son Olger, since he stood as hostage for him. The Emperor at once gave orders that the lad should be put to death; but the keeper of the castle implored the Emperor not to insist upon instant execution, but at least to grant that the young knight should be brought before the Court and told why he must suffer death. To this the Emperor agreed; and as he sat at a great feast among his nobles there entered Olger, and kneeled meekly at his feet. When Charles saw how fair a youth he was, and how gently he humbled himself for his father's pride, he was moved with pity and compassion. Many of the nobles, too, were in favour of the lad, and would have begged the Emperor to save his life; but the rage of the messengers was so great that they

would have torn him to pieces, had not Duke Naymes of Bayiere kept them back.

Then Olger looked up at the Emperor, and said:

"Sire, you know that I am innocent in this matter, and that I have always been obedient to you. Let me not suffer for my father's fault, but, since I am his true heir, let me pay the homage and allegiance which he refuses, and grant that I may atone for him by a life of devotion and service in your cause. And for your messengers, I will from this moment do all in my power to recompense them for the cruel indignities they have suffered at my father's hands, if you will but spare my life and use it in your service."

Then all the barons began to beg the King to grant the boy's request; and in the midst of the discussion a mounted knight rode into the hall, crying:

"Tidings, my lord King! Ill tidings for us all! The Soudan and the Grand Turk and Dannemont his son, with the help of King Caraheu, have taken Rome by storm, and Pope, cardinals, and all have fled. The churches are destroyed; the Christians put to the sword. Wherefore, as a Christian king and pillar of the Faith, I summon you to march to the aid of Holy Church."

Then, as all was bustle and confusion in preparing a great army to take the field immediately, Duke Naymes prevailed upon Charles to let him take young Olger to the battle as his squire, promising to give all his lands, and himself as prisoner, to the Emperor, if the boy should flee away. So Charles agreed, and hastened to prepare for the fight, swearing that he would not return to his own land till Rome should be restored to the Christians. The first thing Olger did when he recovered his freedom, was to hasten back to the castle and wed the fair Bellisande; and when she wept at losing her young husband so soon, he comforted her, and said: "Weep not, for God has

given me life and you have given me love—and these two gifts will strengthen me to do great feats of arms."

So Olger rode off with the host, following the standard of Duke Naymes and his two brothers, Geoffrey and Gautier. And they marched till they came to Rome, and took their station on a hill before the city with an army of two hundred thousand men.

Then the host of paynims came forth from the city to the battle; and Olger, hearing the din of war, the neighing of horses, and the shouting of men, longed to dash into the thick of the fight; but his master forbade him, and charged him to remain among the tents.

From this position Olger watched with wild anxiety the standard of King Charles as it waved in the forefront of the battle. He saw the armies come together and heard a crash that rent the sky. Then the standard waved in triumph; but suddenly it fell, then rose again; and anon he saw with horror that the band of the Emperor's chosen knights had been repulsed, and that Sir Alory, the standard-bearer, had turned his horse, and was fleeing for his very life. In a moment Olger had rushed down the slope, and, flinging himself on the bridle of Sir Alory's horse, he snatched the standard from his hand, crying: "Coward, go home with all the speed you may, and live among women for the rest of your life, but leave the noble banner, Refuge of France, with me."

The terrified Alory was easily disarmed; and Olger, ordering a squire to dress him in the standard-bearer's armour, sprang on a horse and, sword in one hand and banner in the other, rushed into the thick of the fight.

He soon found that Duke Naymes and many other nobles had been held prisoners behind the array of the paynims, and, with the fierceness of a young lion, he cut his way through to them, freed their bonds with his sword, and forced a

way through the enemy both for himself and for them. And wherever he appeared among the heathen host, he slew so many that he was protected, as it were, by a rampart of the dead. Presently he heard the King cry loudly for help, and, spurring in the direction of the sound, found that Dannemont had killed his horse under him, and that he was down, and hard pressed on every side. Then Olger, waving the standard on high, rushed upon the paynim, and soon cleared a free space about the King, and mounted him on a fresh horse. And in the same way on three separate occasions he saved the life of Charles. At length, with Olger at their head and the battle-cry of "Montjoy" on their lips, the King and his host drove the paynims back to the city gates.

When the fight was over, the Emperor Charles ordered the standard-bearer to be brought before him; and when Olger appeared, with his visor closed, he thought it had been Alory, and said to him: "Alory, though with grief I saw you flee at the onset, you have most nobly redeemed your honour. Three times have you saved my life, and I know not how to reward you fitly. I will make you ruler of any province you may choose in my kingdom, and you shall be my lieutenant, and fight in my quarrel in all disputes touching the crown of France."

But a squire who stood by spoke up, and said: "Sire, this is not that Alory of whom you speak. He bowed the colours, and fled for his life, at the first onset; but this young knight seized the standard from his hands, while I helped to dress him in Alory's armour; but who he is I know not."

Then Olger took off his helmet, and knelt down, and said: "Have pity, sire, on Godfrey, King of Denmark, and let his son atone for his offence and be your faithful vassal in his stead."

And the Emperor embraced him, and said: "You have changed all former hate into love for you. I give you your

request. Rise, Sir Olger, Champion for France and Charles, and God be with you."

Thus Olger became a knight, and all the nobles of France came to salute him and thank him for their deliverance. On the next day, proud in his new-made knighthood, Olger once more bore the standard against the foe, and the paynims fell like corn before the scythe wherever he appeared. And when the Franks began to waver, then there rode into their midst a knight on a great horse, who did such mighty deeds on their behalf that they knew him for their Champion, and crying: "Olger! Olger the Dane!" they made many a mighty charge upon the foe.

When Sadonne, the paynim general, heard that the tide of battle was going against his army, he rode forth to meet his followers with the news that Caraheu, Emperor of India, with thirty kings, was coming to their aid. But soon he met the whole array fleeing, panic-stricken, towards him in full flight, and crying, "Save yourselves, for Michael the Archangel fights against us!" Then, before Sadonne had time to flee, his path was crossed by the dread knight on the great horse, and at once he threw down his arms, and begged for life.

"What is your name?" said Sir Olger.

"I am Sadonne," answered he, "the general of Caraheu, Emperor of India."

"On one condition only will I grant you your life," said Sir Olger: "You must bear to Caraheu my challenge to fight with me in single combat, so that by this the course of the war may be determined."

So Sadonne departed, and next day Caraheu arrived at the pavilion of Charles the Emperor with a gorgeous retinue, and with him he brought the beautiful Gloriande, the fairest lady in all the Eastern world. Her hair was like spun gold, and fell to her feet like a cloak. It was bound about her temples by a

jewelled circlet of the rarest gems, and her dress, of whitest damask sewn with pearls, had taken full nine years to weave.

Then Caraheu the Emperor said: "I am in search of Olger the Dane, who has demanded single combat with me. His challenge I accept, and fair Gloriande, my promised bride, shall be the victor's prize."

But Charlot, son of the Emperor Charles, looked with envy on Olger, and said: "'Tis meet that you, great Caraheu, should fight, not with my father's bondsman, but with me."

"Not I," replied the Emperor. "I fight not with braggarts, but with men. Sir Olger rules the hearts of men, which is nobler far than ruling over lands."

"Nay, Emperor," said Olger modestly; "Charlot here is the Emperor's son, and worthy to fight with the highest."

"Let him fight with Sadonne, my general," said Caraheu. "I will joust only with you."

So a double combat was arranged, and Gloriande sat in a place from which she could strengthen the combatants with the glances of her bright eyes. For half a day they fought without either getting the upper hand, until Sadonne killed Charlot's horse, and courteously leapt from his own in order to fight upon equal terms. But the base-minded Charlot only pretended to fight until he reached the place where Sadonne's steed was standing, and, leaping on it, he rode away, like a coward and recreant knight.

Meantime the good sword of Caraheu had cut through Sir Olger's shield and armour, and would have done worse harm had not the knight with his great strength dragged Caraheu from his horse, and disarmed him. But Dannemont, the paynim, had hidden three hundred men among the bushes of that place to see how the combat went. And when he saw Caraheu at Olger's mercy, he rushed forth at the head of his men, and began to attack the knight. In vain did Caraheu rail

at them for their treachery, and fight with all his strength on Olger's side, crying: "Shame on ye, traitors! Better death than this!" Numbers overpowered them, and Olger's life was only saved at the request of the fair Gloriande. He was loaded with chains, and thrown into a dungeon, in spite of all that Caraheu could say or do on his behalf. At length, angry and disgusted at this foul blot on his honour, the latter left the paynim army, and went over with all his men to the side of the Emperor Charles, determined to go on fighting against the paynim until Olger was delivered. But Gloriande, who, according to the fairy gift, had loved Olger from the first moment she saw him, went in secret to his prison, loosed his chains, and let him escape to the camp of Charles. Then Charles and Olger and Caraheu joined together against the paynim host, and ere long Rome was freed from her enemies. Then Olger rescued Gloriande, and gave her to Caraheu to be his wife. In Rome were they baptised and married, and returned to India a Christian man and woman. But ere he departed, he gave to Olger his famous sword, Courtain, saying: "My life and my bride both have you won, and both you have given back to me; take, therefore, this sword as a pledge that I owe all to you."

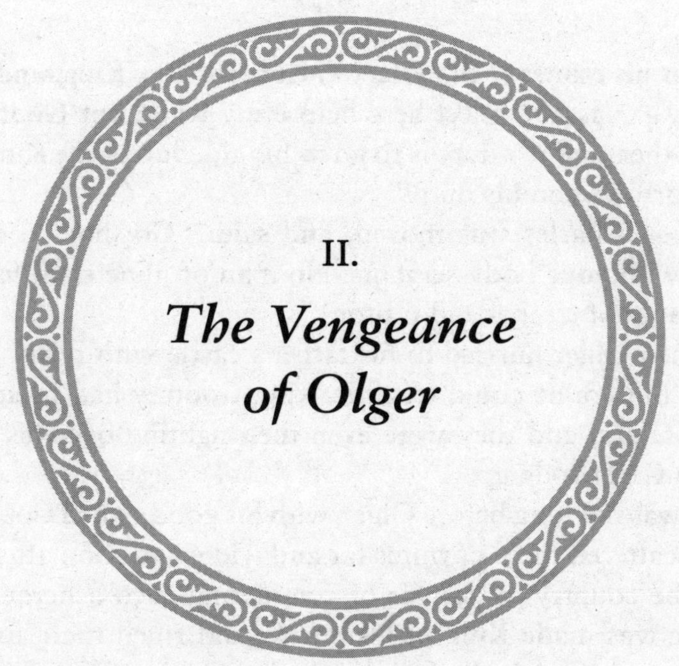

## II.
# *The Vengeance of Olger*

When Olger returned to France he found that his wife was dead. This grieved him very sorely, but he was comforted somewhat by the sight of the little son who had been born to him meantime. And he called his name Baldwin.

Now, at this time the paynims had come down upon Denmark, and had harried all the land. And they shut up King Godfrey in his own castle, and besieged it so that he nearly died of famine. Then the Queen said: "Surely this trouble is come upon us for Olger's sake, whom we left to die." And they began to repent of their wickedness, until at length, becoming very low and miserable, they sent a message to King Charles, begging him to forgive them, and to send them help. But the Emperor replied: "No! Since Godfrey holds his lands of God and of his good sword, let him hold them. I will not lift a hand to help him." Then he sent for Olger, and said: "You would not wish to help a traitor—one, too, who left you to

die for his crimes?" But Olger knelt before the King, and said: "Sire, as vassal I kneel here before my King; but Godfrey is my father, and my duty is to go to his aid. Surely the King will not forbid a son his duty!"

Then Charles was moved, and said: "Go; but go alone, save with your body-servants. No man of mine shall fight in the cause of a rebel and traitor."

Then Olger hurried to his father's castle with thirty of his men; but ere he could reach it, King Godfrey had been slain by his foes, and they were even then fighting over his body when Olger rode up.

It was not long before Olger, with his good sword Courtain, had scattered these paynims far and wide, and soon after they left the country in despair of conquering such a hero. Then Olger was made King of Denmark, and ruled there for five years; and when he had settled the land and made good laws, he returned to the Emperor Charles, and, kneeling before him, said: "The son of Godfrey, of his own free will, thus pays homage to King Charles for all the land of Denmark."

The King embraced him warmly at these words, and begged him to remain as long as possible at the Frankish Court. Now, one day the little Baldwin, Olger's son, a fair-headed child whom all good men looked upon with favour, was playing chess with Charlot, son of the Emperor; and it came to pass that, having quickly given "fool's mate" to the prince, the boy began to laugh at him for his bad play.

Then Charlot, who had always hated Olger, and was jealous of young Baldwin, took up the heavy chessboard, and beat the child on the head, so that he fell lifeless to the ground.

When Olger returned from the hunt and found his little son lying dead, he was beside himself with grief. He covered the child with tears and kisses, and then, making his way to the Emperor's presence, he laid the boy before his throne, saying:

"Sire, look upon your son's foul deed."

The Emperor was sorely grieved; but he tried to comfort Olger, saying he would give half his kingdom if it would bring the child to life again, but that he knew well that nothing could make up for such a loss.

Then Olger said very sternly: "There is no compensation, but there is punishment to be given. Grant me now to fight with your son, and so avenge my poor child's death."

"Nay," said the Emperor, "for how, then, could he have a chance of life?"

"What matters that?" cried Olger, with bitter look. "What is your son more than mine? I demand that he be given up to me."

"I cannot do it," said the Emperor.

"Then," cried Olger in great wrath, "till you learn justice, sire, we part company." And forthwith he left the Court, and took service with a Lombard king who was fighting against King Charles.

For the next few years Olger the Dane won great renown by his warfare against the Franks, for wherever he went he was always the victor, and his enemies began to look upon his good sword Courtain, and Broiefort, his great black steed, with awe and terror. Many of the Franks said openly, that to let Olger depart and to make him their foe, had been no wise deed, for he came upon them like a blight upon the summer corn. At length they made a plot against him, and determined to get the better of him by foul treachery. So they watched him privily, and found him one day, tired out with fighting, lying fast asleep by a fountain, with his arms scattered far and wide, and his good steed Broiefort grazing peacefully by his side. Then one seized his horse, and another his weapons, and they bound him fast while he still lay sound asleep.

When Sir Olger was brought to the Court as a prisoner, the Emperor wished to slay him, because he feared the vengeance of Olger on his son, and in return for the harm he had done to the Frankish cause. But the knights and barons would not hear of this, saying that they had lent themselves to treachery to save their native land, but that the life of the noblest knight in Christendom should not be lost thereby. So he was put into prison, and kept under a strong guard for several years.

Now, after these days did Achar, King of England, land in France to do homage to the Emperor for his lands; and with him came his fair daughter Clarice. But as he journeyed to the Court a certain Saracen giant named Bruhier arrived with a great army to make war upon the Franks, and he seized the persons of Achar and his daughter, and marched to fight against the Emperor. And so great was the power of this giant that the Frankish army could not stand before him, but fled before his face. Then the barons and knights began to implore Charles to release Olger from his prison and prevail on him to fight for them, and forthwith the Emperor went himself ta the prison to implore his aid. But Olger would not listen for a moment to this proposal, unless the Emperor would first deliver Charlot the prince into his hands. For a long time the Emperor would not agree to this; but at length his whole army reproached him, saying: "Have you no care for us that you let us die by thousands in a hopeless fight? Why should a thousand die for one?"

So Charles was forced to deliver up his son.

Then, as Charlot begged and prayed for mercy, Olger thought only of his fair-haired little boy, and, taking the prince by the hair, raised Courtain to strike off his head. But as he did so a voice from the air cried: "Stay thy hand, Olger the Dane! Slay not the son of the King!" and at the same moment vivid flashes of lightning came about them both. Then the

sword fell from Olger's hand, and all who had heard the voice trembled and greatly feared. The King, in his joy at the deliverance of his son, would have poured out his gratitude to the Dane, but Olger only said: "Your thanks are due to God, not to me. I do but bow to His will." And that day the King and Olger were made friends.

But when the Dane would have made ready to fight against the Saracen, he found that nothing had been heard or seen of his good horse Broiefort for seven long years, and all men believed him to be dead. The Emperor sent him his best charger in his stead, but scarcely had the knight leaped into the saddle when the creature fell beneath his weight. Ten other of the finest horses in the land were tried, and, finding that none could carry him, Olger declared that he must go afoot. But a certain man was found who said he had seen the horse Broiefort dragging blocks of stone for the building of the Abbey of St Meaux, and immediately a little band rode off to bring the horse back to his master. They found him but skin and bone, his hair worn off his sides, his tail shorn to the stump, his skin galled by the shafts, a very scarecrow of a horse, yet dragging a load that four other horses could not stir. They brought him to Olger with all speed; and when the sturdy knight leaned upon him, he did not cringe under the weight, but straightened himself, and, knowing his master, snorted and neighed with joy, and pawed the ground, and knelt down humbly before him on the grass.

So Olger went to battle upon Broiefort, and wherever he went he won the day. He slew the giant Bruhier, drove the Saracen from the land, and rescued King Achar, and his daughter Clarice, whom the King of Britain gave him for his wife. And when they were married, they crossed the sea, and Achar made Olger King of Britain in his stead. For many years he ruled this country, and there his faithful Broiefort died

and was buried. At length he grew weary of peace, and went to fight for the Holy Cross in Palestine; and there he fought many a hard battle, and won many a victory, till he was old and grey with years. Then he left the Holy Land, and set sail for France that he might see Charles the Great and his Court once more before he returned to Britain, there to end his days.

But on that journey there came upon them a great storm; and the tempestuous wind drove the ship in which Olger was far away from the rest, into strange seas, without rudder, oars, or mast; and a strong current seized the vessel, and crashed it against a reef of loadstone rock. All who were on board leaped into the waves, and were soon dashed lifeless against the beach; only Sir Olger remained upon the deck in the black darkness, gazing out upon the stormy sea. He bared his head, and, drawing Courtain, kissed the crossed hilt, and thanked God for the courage given him as a soldier all his life, and then quietly awaited death.

III.

## *The Return from Avalon*

Darker and wilder grew the night, when, just as the waves seemed about to overwhelm the ship, a voice from the air cried, clear and strong: "Olger, I wait for thee. Come, and fear not the waves." And immediately he cast himself into the sea, and was borne on the crest of a great billow high up in the air, and placed in safety among the rocks. A weird light shone through the gloom, and showed a narrow pathway through the crags, and, following this, Olger presently saw a brilliant glow in front of him, which gradually took the shape of a shining palace, which none can see by day, but which at nightfall glows with unearthly splendour. Its walls were of ivory, inlaid with gold and ebony, and within its spacious hall was set a most rare banquet upon a golden table. But the only inhabitant of the palace was a fairy horse named Papillon, who signed to Olger to seat himself at the banquet, and brought him water in a golden pitcher for his

hands, and served him at table while he ate. When he had finished, Papillon carried him off to a bed, in the pillars of which stood golden candlesticks, wherein wax tapers burned the whole night through.

So Olger slept; but when he awoke next day, the fairy palace had vanished in the morning light, and he found himself lying in a fair garden, where the trees were always green and the flowers unfading and the summer never comes to an end, where no storm ever darkens the sweet, soft sky, and the chill of sunset is not known. For it was a garden in the vale of Avalon, in Fairyland.

And as he gazed around him, greatly wondering, there appeared at his side Morgan le Fay, Queen of the Fairies, clothed in shining white apparel, and said to him: "Welcome, dear knight, to Avalon. Long have I waited and wearied for your coming. Now you are mine for ever. The ages may roll away, and the world fall to pieces; we will dream for ever in this vale, where all things are the same." Then she put an enchanted ring on his finger, and immediately he became a youth again, beautiful and vigorous. And on his head she placed a crown of myrtle leaves and laurel, all in gold; and Olger remembered no more his former life, for she had given him the Crown of Forgetfulness.

So Olger sojourned in that fair land; and there he met and talked with King Arthur, healed now of his mortal wound, and the forms of Sir Lancelot and Sir Tristram and of many other noble knights of the Table Bound.

And so two hundred years passed by like a beautiful dream.

Meantime sad events had taken place in the land of France. No great leader had arisen after Charles the Great, and the land had fallen into poverty and shame. Everywhere the Franks were beaten back by Paynim and by Saracen, and chivalry seemed lost for ever. In vain the people cried out for a

deliverer; and at length Morgan le Fay heard and pitied them. So she went to Olger the Dane, and said to him:

"Dear knight, how long have you dwelt here with me?"

"It may be a week, a month, or perchance a year," he answered, smiling, "for I have lost all count of time."

Then Morgan le Fay lifted the Crown of Forgetfulness from his brows, and at once his memory came to him again.

"I must go back," he cried, as though awaking from sleep. "Too long have I tarried here. Clarice will be calling for me, and Charles, my master, will have summoned Olger in vain. Where is my sword, my horse! Now let me go, fair queen, but tell me first how long I have dwelt here."

"It seems not long to me, dear knight," said she; "but you shall go when you will."

Then Morgan le Fay brought to life again his dead squire Benoist, and brought out Courtain, his good sword, and led forth Papillon for his steed. "Keep safe the ring upon your hand," said she, "for so long as you wear it, youth and vigour shall not fail you. And take also this torch, but see you light it not, for so long as it remains unlighted your life is safe; but, if ever it should begin to burn, guard the flame well, for with the last spark of the torch shall your days end."

She wove, moreover, a spell about them, so that they fell into a deep sleep. And when Sir Olger awoke, he found himself lying by a fountain, with his sword and armour near by, and Benoist holding Papillon ready for him to mount. Leaping on their horses, they rode along till, not far from a town, they overtook a horseman.

"What city is this, good sir?" asked Olger.

"Montpellier," answered the man.

"Ah, yes; I had forgotten," said Olger. "Yet I ought to know well enough, for a kinsman of mine is governor there." And he named the man whom he believed to be the governor.

"You are strangely in error," said the horseman, "though I remember now to have heard there was a ruler of that name two hundred years ago. He was a great writer of romances, and I daresay you know, since you claim him as your ancestor, that he wrote the romance of Olger the Dane. A good story enough, though, of course, no one believes it now, save perhaps one man, who often sings it about the city, and picks up money from the passers-by." Then he fell back a few paces, and riding beside Benoist, said to him: "Who is your master?"

"Surely you must know him," said the squire, "he is Olger the Dane."

"Rascal!" cried the stranger, "you are making a jest of me. All men know that Olger the Dane perished in shipwreck two hundred years ago. That is a fine story indeed!" And he rode away.

The knight and his squire pursued their journey till they came to the market-place of Meaux, where they stopped at the door of an inn well known to them in former days.

"Can we lodge here?" asked Olger.

"Certainly you can," replied the innkeeper.

"Then fetch the landlord to speak with me."

"Sir," said the man, "I am the landlord."

"Nay, nay," said Olger; "I wish to see Hubert the Neapolitan, the landlord of this house."

The man gave him one look, and then, taking him for a madman, bolted the door in his face, and, rushing to an upper window, cried: "Seize that horseman for a madman. He asks to see Hubert, my grandfather's grandfather, who has been dead two hundred years. Send for the Abbot of St Faron, that he may drive out the evil spirit from him."

Then a crowd began to gather, and stones and darts were hurled at the knight and his man, and in the scuffle that followed Benoist was shot dead by an archer. And when Sir

Olger saw that, he was filled with the fiercest wrath, and rode Papillon at the crowd, and scattered them, cutting down with his sword all who came within reach. But so hotly burnt his wrath that it kindled the torch that he carried in his breast, so he rode away with it to the Abbey of St Faron. There the Abbot met him, to whom Olger said: "Is your name Simon? You at least should know me, seeing that I founded this abbey and endowed it with lands and money." But the Abbot answered that he knew little of those who had preceded him, and asked the stranger's name. And when he heard it he was greatly puzzled, and said to himself: "I do remember me that the charters of the house say that Simon was Abbot in the days of the founder, Olger the Dane; yet what does all this mean?" And aloud he said: "Sir Knight, the Abbot Simon has been buried for nigh two hundred years."

"What!" cried the knight. "Simon dead! And Charles the Great and Caraheu and Clarice, my wife? Where are they? Not dead too? Oh, say they are not dead!"

"Dead, dead two hundred years ago, my son," said the Abbot solemnly. Then Sir Olger was filled with awe and wonder, as he began to realise that his dream of Avalon was true after all. Following the Abbot into the church he told his strange story, and the Abbot believed him, and rejoiced to think that a deliverer had been sent to France at last. Then Olger told him the secret of the torch, and begged him to make an iron treasure-house beneath the church, wherein so little air could come that the flame might dwindle to a single spark, and yet be nourished and preserved for many years to come. And when this was done, and the torch was safely disposed of, the Abbot begged to see the magic ring. But when Olger heedlessly drew it from his finger, immediately his youth and vigour vanished, and he became a helpless old man, whose skin hung loose like withered parchment, and

whose only sign of life was the quivering of his toothless jaws. The terrified Abbot hastily put back the ring on the fleshless finger, and immediately Olger's strength and youth returned, and he rode off on Papillon to fight for France. The enemy was then stationed before Chartres, and so strong they were that the Franks were falling back disheartened before them, when suddenly, just as in former days, a gigantic knight riding a coal-black horse appeared in their midst, and everywhere he rode was marked by a long line of slain. Then the astonished Franks remembered the stories they had heard in the days of old, and murmured to one another: "It is Olger the Dane!" One after the other passed it on, till the murmur grew to a cry, and the cry to a shout of "Olger! Olger the Dane!" and, rushing upon the foe, they swept the paynims from the field. Over and over again did Olger thus lead the Franks to victory, until at length the land was free. And always while he fought the torch burned bright in the Church of St Faron, but when he rested it dwindled to a spark again.

At length the renowned and glorious knight had leisure to visit the French Court. He found that the King of France had lately died, but the Queen received him with all kindness; and her waiting maid, the Lady of Senlis, loved him so much that she would gladly have wedded him, but he would have nothing to do with her. Now, one day these ladies discovered the secret of the magic ring; for, finding him one day asleep upon a couch after a long journey, they drew the ring from his finger, meaning to jest with him about it when he awoke. Much to their horror, the strong man withered up before their eyes, and became an ancient skeleton.

Then the Queen, knowing from this that it was truly Olger the Dane, immediately replaced the ring, and he regained his former youth. But the Lady of Senlis, determined that since Olger did not care for her, he should love no one else, sent

thirty strong knights to waylay him as he left the Court, and to wrest the ring of Morgan le Fay from his hand. But Sir Olger spurred Papillon among them, with Courtain drawn in his hand, and so escaped untouched. After this the Queen herself wished to marry Olger, for she said: "He, and he alone, is worthy to sit upon the throne of Charles the Great." And to this Olger agreed, for he felt to sit in his master's seat was the highest earthly honour he could win. So with great pomp and ceremony they prepared for the wedding. The great church blazed with golden banners as a lordly procession entered and proclaimed the approaching coronation of the new-made King; and Sir Olger took the Queen by the hand, and led her forward, and knelt with her upon the chancel pavement. But ere the marriage vows were spoken, a brighter light than any on earth shone upon them, and all at once a thick white cloud wrapped round the knight. Some say that Morgan le Fay was seen floating down through the cloud, with arms outstretched, to carry off her knight. However that may be, when the cloud had cleared away Sir Olger was no more to be seen upon this earth. But men whisper that Olger the Dane lives yet, for the torch still burns in the treasure-house of the Abbey of St Faron. He is only asleep in the faery islands of Avalon, and one day he will awaken, and return again, return to deliver France once more in time of need, when the Franks shall turn, and conquer their foes, with their ancient battle-cry of "Olger! Olger the Dane!"

*From the Anglo-Norman Romance of Charlemagne, about the twelfth century, but undoubtedly borrowed from a Celtic source, since the whole spirit of the tale is Celtic in origin.*

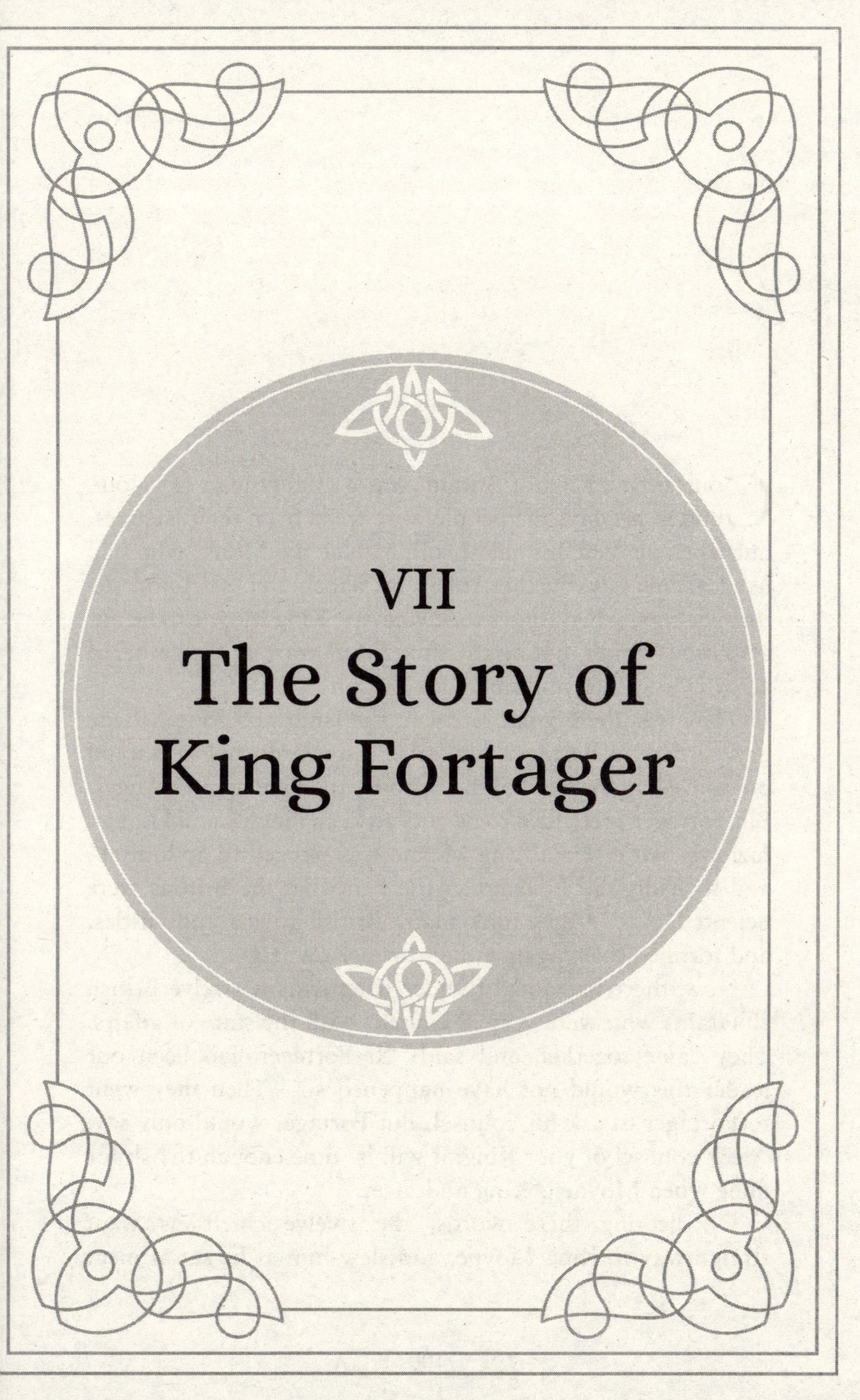

# VII
# The Story of King Fortager

Constaunce, King of Britain, was a mighty man of valour, and in his days the people were freed from their enemies, but when he died, his eldest son, Moyne the Monk, who had lived all his days in the Abbey of Winchester, sat upon the throne. Now when Angys the Dane saw King Moyne to be but a studious youth, hating the thought of warfare, he gathered an army together, and sailed for Britain.

Then was there great terror in the land; and King Moyne gave orders to Fortager, his father's steward, that he should put himself at the head of the Britons, and fight against Angys. But Fortager pretended to be very sick, so that he could not go forth to battle. Then King Moyne was obliged to go himself, and so badly did he conduct the fight that the Britons were defeated. And Angys took many British towns and castles, and fortified them against their former owners.

Now, there had fought under King Moyne twelve British chieftains who were very ill content with the state of affairs. They came together, and said: "If Fortager had been our leader this would not have happened so." Then they went to Fortager to ask his counsel. But Fortager would only say: "Seek counsel of your King; it will be time enough to ask for mine when Moyne is King no longer."

On hearing these words, the twelve chieftains went straightway to King Moyne, and slew him as he sat at meat

within his hall; after which they returned to Fortager, and greeted him as King. But there were many who yet loved the race of good King Constaunce, and some of the barons took his two young sons, Aurilis-Brosias and Uther-Pendragon, the brothers of King Moyne, and sent them away to Brittany, lest they too should be slain.

Meantime Fortager had called together a great army, and had fought with Angys and driven him from the land; and he would have killed the Dane as he prepared to flee, had not Angys begged for mercy and promised to make war no more on Britain.

So Angys sailed away with his host, and Fortager marched in triumph to the capital. And while he was feasting in the palace, the twelve chieftains who had slain King Moyne came to him, and said: "O King, remember it was we who made you King and placed you here on high; give us now a reward." And Fortager answered: "Now that I am King I will indeed give a meet reward for traitors." And, having ordered wild horses to be brought in, he watched them tear the traitors limb from limb upon his castle pavement.

Now, by this deed Fortager roused the wrath of all who had helped him to his throne, and many spoke of bringing back Aurilis-Brosias and Uther-Pendragon to the land. And Fortager was hunted through the kingdom, and sorely beaten, so that he scarce escaped with his life.

At length he determined to send for help to King Angys, which he forthwith did, promising him half the kingdom if he would come to his aid. So Angys returned again with many men and ships, and by his aid Britain was subdued by force of arms. But though the war ceased there was no peace in the land; and Fortager went about in deadly fear, first of the Britons whom he had betrayed, and next of Angys, lest with his powerful host he should seize the whole kingdom. And

lastly, he feared that the men of Brittany would come over and fight for Aurilis-Brosias and Uther-Pendragon, and bring them back to their father's throne.

So he determined to build a strong castle, made of well-hewn stone and timber—an impregnable fortress with lofty towers and battlements, a deep moat and heavy drawbridge—such as had never been seen for strength in the world before; and he decided to rear it on Salisbury Plain, and so be surrounded by wastes of land, and far from his foes. At daybreak three thousand men began the work—hewers of wood and carpenters and masons and cunning workers in stone. The foundations were laid deep, on vast blocks of stone clamped with iron; and by nightfall the wall had risen breast-high. But when they came to their work next morning, they found to their dismay that the ground was scattered with the stones they had built up, and that all they had done was destroyed. That day they built it up again, laying the foundations deeper than before, and clamping each stone to the next with iron. But when they came next morning all was overthrown as before.

Then Fortager called together ten wise men, and shut them in a tower, open to the sky, that they might read the stars, and find out why these things should be. And after nine days the wise men came to him, and said:

"Sire, we read in the stars that an elf child has been born in Britain, knowing things past and things to come. Find the child, and slay him on this plain, and mix the mortar with his blood, and so shall the wall stand fast."

So Fortager sent men forth to journey far and wide till they should find the child, and after wandering for many days and weeks, one party of messengers came to a certain town, and found some children quarrelling in the market-place at their games.

"Thou son of a black elf," they heard one say, "we will not play with thee, for we know not who thou art." The messengers gazed hard at the five-year-old child thus addressed; and immediately the boy, who was called Merlin, ran up to them, and said: "Welcome, O messengers, and behold him whom you seek. But think not, for all men may say, that my blood will ever make firm the castle walls of Fortager; for his wise men who try to read the stars are but blind, and they blunder past what lies at their very feet."

Then the men wondered greatly, and said: "How didst thou know of our errand?"

And Merlin answered: "I can see as it were pictures of all that is and all that shall be. I will go with you to Fortager, and show what hinders building up his fortress on the Plain."

So he mounted a pony, and followed after the men on horseback.

And as they journeyed through a town, they saw a man buying strong new shoes and leather wherewith to mend them when they wore out; and Merlin laughed to himself.

"Why do you laugh?" asked the messengers.

"Because he will never wear the shoes," replied the boy. And so it came to pass, for the man fell dead at his door as he carried home the shoes.

And next day Merlin laughed again, and, being asked why, said: "King Fortager is jealous because his Queen's chamberlain is better looking than he, and he threatens to take his life, knowing not that the handsome fellow is but a woman in disguise."

And when they came to the palace, they found that it was just as the boy had said, so the chamberlain's life was spared. Then Fortager marvelled greatly at the wisdom of this child of five years, and begged him to reveal the mystery of his castle wall. And Merlin said: "The fiends have deceived your wise

men by showing false signs among the stars; for my kindred of the air are very wroth because I have been baptised into Christendom, and they seek to destroy my life. But if you send your men to dig a yard beneath the wall's foundation, they will there find a stream of water running over two mighty stones, under which live two dragons. Each night at sundown these dragons wake, and do battle, so that the earth is shaken, and the wall falls down."

Then Fortager set his men to dig beneath the foundations as Merlin had said; and presently they came to a fast and furious stream, which they turned off by making another channel. And in the river-bed were two huge stones, which it took many men to heave up, and there beneath them lay the dragons. One was as red as fire, and his body a rood in length, with eyes that gleamed like red-hot coals, and a strong and supple tail. The other was milk-white, and very grim of look; he had two heads, and darted out white fire from his jaws. And at sight of them, as they awoke from slumber, all save Merlin fled in panic.

Then the dragons arose, and began to fight. And soon the air was full of the fiery breath from their throats, so that it was like lightning on the earth, and the whole land shook with their noise and fury. All that long summer night they fought with tooth and nail and claw, and fell and rose, and fell and rose again, till the day dawned. And by that time the red dragon had driven the white into a valley, where for a while the latter stood at bay; but at length, recovering himself, he forced the red dragon back into the plain again, and, fixing his claws in his throat, tore him to pieces, and with his fiery flame scorched him up to a heap of ashes on the plain. Then the white dragon flew away into the air.

From that time Merlin became a great favourite of King Fortager, and counselled him in all things. And now, when the

masons began to build, the wall no longer fell down as before, and in course of time a fair white castle arose upon the plain, stronger and mightier than any that the world had ever seen.

Then Fortager sent for Merlin, and asked what the battle of the dragons really meant, and if it betokened things that should yet come to pass. But the boy would answer nothing. Then in his anger King Fortager threatened to slay him; but Merlin only laughed in scorn, saying: "You will never see my death-day. Strike if you will, and bind me fast, but you will only fight the air."

Then Fortager began to entreat him humbly, and swore that no harm should come to him whatever he should say. And at length Merlin told him that the red dragon betokened Fortager and the power he had obtained through killing King Moyne. The white dragon with the two heads represented the true heirs, Aurilis-Brosias and Uther-Pendragon, whose kingdom he held, and as the white dragon, hunted to the valley, there regained his breath, and drove back the red dragon to the plain, so should these heirs, driven out to Brittany, find help and succour there, and were even now sailing to Britain with a vast army to hunt King Fortager through the land, and to drive him to his castle on the Plain. And there, while he was shut up, with his wife and children, he should be burnt to ashes.

Then King Fortager, when he heard this, was grieved at heart, and prayed Merlin to tell him how to avoid this terrible fate, or at least how he might escape with his life. But Merlin only answered: "What will be, will be."

Then Fortager, in his wrath, tried to seize the boy; but Merlin vanished from his sight, and while they sought him, he was all the time far away in the cell of Blaise the hermit. And there he remained for many a year, and wrote a book concerning all the things that were going to happen in Britain.

Meantime all that he had foretold took place. For Uther-Pendragon and his brother marched to Winchester with an army, and when the citizens saw the banner of their old British kings, they drove out the Danish garrison, and opened the gates to the sons of Constaunce. And not one of the men of Britain would fight on the side of Fortager or Angys, nor would the men of their armies fight against their friends and brothers in the land. So they won an easy victory, and drove Fortager away to his fortress on Salisbury Plain, where he shut himself up with his wife and children. And the men of Britain threw wildfire on the walls, and burnt him there, and all that belonged to him, and made his castle walls level with the ground.

But Angys fled away to a fortress on a hill, whither Uther-Pendragon followed, but could not come to him because of the strong bulwarks by which it was surrounded.

Then, hearing men speak often of the wisdom of Merlin, Uther-Pendragon sent men far and wide to seek him. And one day, when these messengers sat at dinner, there came in to them an old beggar, with a snow-white beard and ragged shoes and a staff in his hand, and said: "Ye are wise messengers who seek the child Merlin! Often to-day have ye passed him on the road, and yet ye knew him not. Go back to Uther, and tell him that Merlin waits in the wood hard by; for, search as ye will, ye will never find him."

And with these words the old man disappeared. Then the messengers, wondering greatly, returned, and told all to Uther, who left his brother to maintain the siege, and went to the wood to seek Merlin. And first he met a swineherd, who said he had lately seen the elf child, and then a chapman with his pack, who said the same. Then came a countryman, who said that Merlin would surely keep his tryst, but that Uther must be patient, as he still had some work to do ere he sought the palace.

So the prince waited patiently far into the night; and at length the countryman returned to him, saying: "I am Merlin, and I will now go with you to the camp."

When they got there Aurilis-Brosias came out to meet them, and said: "Brother, there came a countryman in the night, who waked me, saying: 'Angys is come out of his fortress, and has stolen past your sentinels, and is in your camp, seeking to take your life.' So I sprang up, and, seeing Angys at the door, I rushed upon him, and slew him, my sword passing through his coat of mail as if it had been naught. But when all was over, the countryman had vanished."

Then Uther answered: "Brother, here is the countryman, and he is Merlin." Then were the princes much rejoiced, and thanked Merlin for his timely aid. And in the morning the Danes and Saxons yielded up their citadel, and asked leave to sail away to their own land.

So the country was once more free; and the Britons took Uther-Pendragon, the elder of the brothers, and crowned him King at Winchester.

For seven long years he reigned and prospered; and Merlin was counsellor not only to him, but to his son, the great King Arthur, after him.

Amongst the deeds which were performed by the magician to please the King, it is told:

> "How Merlin, by his skill, and magic's wondrous
> might,
> From Ireland hither brought the Stonendge in a
> night."
>
> — *Drayton*

And many of these stones may still be seen standing upon Salisbury Plain.

# VIII
# Wild Wales

Once upon a time, says a famous Welsh legend, a certain witch named Caridwen set to work to brew a cauldron of knowledge that might make her youngest son the wisest man in the world. Now, this cauldron had to boil for a year and a day, and at the end of that time it would yield three drops of precious liquid which would make whoever drank them the wisest of all men. So she set a passing tramp named Gwion Bach to stir the cauldron and to keep it on the boil, and made up her mind to kill him directly the time was up, lest he should learn the secret of the magic liquid.

But she miscalculated the time, and so it happened that one day, in her absence, the three magic drops flew up out of the cauldron and fell upon the finger of Gwion Bach. Feeling his finger thus scalded, he put it to his mouth and sucked it, and immediately he became very wise, and knew what Caridwen meant to do to him.

So he fled to his own people, and the cauldron, left unstirred, burst in two, so that the poisonous liquid that was left, poured out and flowed into a stream near by, and all the cattle that drank of that stream went mad and died.

When Caridwen saw this, she made haste to catch Gwion Bach and put him to death; but he, when he saw her running after him, changed himself into a hare, for the magic potion had given him skill of all kinds. But she immediately turned herself into a greyhound, and had nearly caught him, when he sprang into a river and changed himself into a fish. Then she became an otter, and chased him till, hard pressed, he took the form of a bird. Caridwen then became a hawk, and chased him till, dead-beat, he fell into a granary and changed himself into a grain of wheat. The witch promptly became a high-crested black hen, and scratched among the grains till she found him. She was about to swallow him, when he, now almost at the end of his resources, became a beautiful little child. Then Caridwen, not having the heart to kill him, put him into a leathern bag and cast him into the sea, not far from Aberystwith, just below the Weir of Gwyddno, on April 29.

Now, Gwyddno had a most unlucky son named Elphin, who was "always needing and never getting"; and in order that he might gain something for himself, his father granted him all the weir should contain on May-day. So the nets were set, but in the morning they were quite empty save for a leathern bag which had caught in one of them. Then said one of his companions: "Till this day, the weir has been worth a hundred pounds' worth of fish every May morning. Now see how your luck has turned them away, and left you nothing but a skin."

"Nay," said Elphin; "perhaps the skin bag may have something in it that is worth more than a hundred pounds."

So they opened it, and a little lad peeped out.

"See what a bright face!" they cried. And Elphin, heavy with disappointment, said, "Let him be called Taliesin, then" (which means Bright Face), and took him home behind him on his horse. But as they rode along the boy began to sing to him so sweet a song of consolation that Elphin marvelled, and asked where he had learnt a thing so beautiful. Then Taliesin replied that, though he was but little, he was, nevertheless, very wise. When they reached the house, Gwyddno asked his

son if he had had a good haul. "Father," replied Elphin, "I have caught a poet-minstrel."

"Alas! What good will that do thee?" asked his father; but Taliesin answered for himself: "It will do him more good than the weir ever did for thee!"

And so it came about; for Taliesin, the magic child, not only saved Elphin's life and liberty when he was in great danger and made him a rich and fortunate man; he also brought high fame to the House of Gwyddno by his very name and connection with it. For Taliesin, the rest of whose wonderful story must be read elsewhere, became the minstrel, and bard, and prophet of the Britain of old days; and this was one of his prophecies made concerning the people of his land:

"Their Lord they shall praise, Their language they shall keep, Their land they shall lose Except Wild Wales."

Let us see how the prophecy has been fulfilled.

When the Romans conquered Britain, they found the hardest part of their task lay in that north-western part of the island which is now called Wales. The people were more uncivilized than the Britons of the south-east, but they knew how to fight to the death; and the Roman writer paints for us a vivid picture of the grim lines of warriors, urged on by the cries of wild women dancing a witch-dance in the van, and by the words of the white-robed, ivy-crowned Druids, who called down the curses of the sky-god upon the Roman foe.

Even when this part of Britain at length was subdued, the inhabitants were very little influenced by their conquerors. They used the fine Roman roads laid down for the passage of their conquerors' troops from Caerleon to Chester and along the coast; they marvelled at the pretty Roman villas that arose upon their borders; but they kept their own language and their own customs, and were influenced scarcely at all by the civilization which was spreading fast in the south and

east of Britain. One thing, however, they eagerly embraced, and that was the Christian faith, and that is one reason why many Welsh words connected with the religious services of the Church are merely Latin words in disguise.

When the rest of Britain, at the end of the fifth century, had fallen into the hands of the English invaders and conquerors, the western part remained free. High among their mountains, these fierce tribes bade defiance to Angle, and Saxon, and Jute, and to them came for protection many of those who had been forced to flee for their lives from other parts of Britain. From that time this region came to be known by the English as *Wales,* the Land of Strangers; and thus was part of the prophecy concerning the whole people of Britain fulfilled:

"*Their land they shall lose Except Wild Wales.*"

"*Their language they shall keep.*" We have seen how few Latin words had been borrowed from the Romans, and now that all the rest of the island was fast forgetting its original tongue and learning the language of its conquerors, the men of the West were fulfilling that part of the prophecy also. Up to this time there had been in the land three distinct races, and at least three languages. There were the short, dark-haired Celts, who came originally from the South of Europe, and who became the serfs of the next new-comers, the Irish Celts. These were tall, red-haired people, and very like them were the next to come, the Brythons, or Welsh Celts. While the English were making themselves masters of the rest of Britain, these two latter tribes were at civil war, and in the end the Brythons, or Britons, got the upper hand, and their language became the language of Wales.

It was about this time, too, that the first line of the bardic prophecy began to be fulfilled. Under the stirring influence of Dewi, the Water-drinker, the monk of Dyfed, whom we know as St. David, Wales became caught up in a wave of

religious zeal. Monasteries were built, missionaries travelled from end to end of the country, everywhere the Gospel was preached, and the people received it gladly. Countless Welsh "saints," or missionaries, arose, whose names are now only remembered by the churches or places dedicated to them; and while England was sunk in heathen darkness, the light of the Celtic Church was burning brightly in the West. From that time down to the present day religious zeal has been the characteristic of the Welshman. "*Their Lord they shall praise.*"

The Norman Conquest, five centuries later, brought the Lowlands of Wales—the Borderland, or "Marches," as it was called—under the rule of Norman barons, but the wilder part of the country, though it condescended to borrow something of Norman civilization, remained independent. At the end of the reign of Henry III. Wales was a land of shepherd farmers, who knew well how to use the bow and the spear. They were divided into many tribes, but united by their religion and by their love of music, poetry, oratory, and all those arts which depend upon a vivid imagination for their growth. Even to this day the stories that they told are as fascinating to us as they were to the Welsh boys and girls who first heard them as they sat by the rude hearthstone, and heard the wind skirling down the mountain outside the heavily barred door.

Fortunately for this Celtic spirit of imagination that turns all it touches to gold, the next attempt at conquest shook rather than shattered the independence of Wild Wales. But we shall best understand and enjoy this part of the story of the land if we read it in connection with the particular places at which the more striking events occurred.

# IX
# The Fastness of Llewelyn

The story of the great struggle of Wales for freedom under a Prince of her own is laid, fitly enough, amid the wild scenery that surrounds the highest point in Southern Britain. The whole district of Snowdon, with its grim moorlands and towering heights forming a bulwark to the western shore, breathes an air of freedom, and it was here that the last Llewelyn defied the might of the first English Edward.

Roused by the bitter lament of those who had fallen under the yoke of the Anglo-Norman barons, Llewelyn, Lord of Snowdon, threw off the pretence of alliance and friendship which Henry III. had thought well to keep up between them, and claimed to be ruler of all Wales, as his grandfather had done in the days of Henry II. During the long Barons' War in England the "Lord of Snowdon" found no difficulty in maintaining his right to be "Prince of Wales"; the real trouble only began when Edward I., on his accession, called upon the Prince to do homage as his vassal. For two years Llewelyn paid no heed, and when he heard that an English army was advancing upon him, went out boldly to meet it.

But the chieftains of Central and South Wales turned traitor, his own brother David deserted him, and the Prince, driven back to the inmost recesses of his mountain fastness, was forced to lay down his arms. Preferring to have him as friend rather than enemy, Edward behaved generously enough,

merely seizing a large slice of his dominions, confining him to the Snowdon district, and providing that the title "Prince of Wales" should cease at his death.

Four years elapsed of outward peace and inward commotion. Then came a rumour of a strange event. Long years before, Merlin, a famous Welsh bard and prophet, had foretold that "when English money became round, a Prince of Wales should be crowned in London." In 1282 a new copper coinage had taken the place of the usual breaking of the silver penny into halves and quarters; and in that same year the traitor David, who had been rewarded with an English earldom, threw off his allegiance to Edward, and appeared with an army before his brother's dwelling-place. Gladly did Llewelyn once more raise the standard of revolt, and a desperate struggle for freedom began. The great army of the English King, encircling the Snowdon range, which was the headquarters of the Prince, drew in closer and closer; but meantime the English soldiers were suffering terribly in that hard winter of 1282, which the hardy Welshmen, living in the snowbound caves of the mountain, seemed to pass through unheeding. As long as Llewelyn was there to inspire and cheer, pain and even death were to be welcomed; but almost by chance the men of Wales lost their leader in a quite unimportant skirmish. Llewelyn had emerged from his mountain lair, and, hoping to drive the English from the Brecknock district, had ridden forth to meet some allies. He was met by a party of English horsemen and cut down by an almost unknown knight. With Llewelyn, "our last ruler," as the Welsh still call him, the cause of Welsh independence was lost. At Rhuddlan, in Flintshire, you may still see a bit of the wall remaining where the Statute of Wales was passed by the Parliament held there in 1284; and in that Statute Edward showed the greatest wisdom; for, instead of forcing English laws and customs upon them, he allowed the

Welsh to keep their own as far as possible, altering them only where it was clearly for their own advantage.

It was at Carnarvon Castle, which guards the entrance to "Snowdonia," that the little Prince was born who was presented by Edward I. to the Welsh chieftains upon a shield as a "Prince of Wales who could not speak a word of English." And nowadays Carnarvon is, perhaps, the best starting-point from which to take a glimpse of this wild and mountainous district.

Behind us, as we look towards the mountains, lie the Menai Straits, spanned by the fine suspension bridge, so strong and yet so fairy-like with its arches of Anglesey marble, that it has been called a "poem in stone and iron." This bridge continues the Holyhead road to the island of Anglesey, the home of the Llewelyns, where the soil is so fertile that an old saying declares that it can provide corn enough for all the people in Wales; and thence, across the island, we may reach Holyhead, the starting-point for the Irish mail-boats.

Travelling towards Snowdon by rail to Llanberis, the scenery changes rapidly from pretty woods and pastures to that of rugged heights, crags, and rock-bound lakes. The mountain valley in which the village lies is commanded by the very ancient Welsh castle of Dolbadarn, once the prison of Owen, the brother of the ill-fated Llewelyn, Lord of Snowdon. Below is the great lake, and beyond the wild Pass of Llanberis, bounded by a "tumultuous chaos of rock and crag, as if Titans in some burst of fury had been rending cliffs and flinging their fragments far and wide." If we are lazy, we may climb Snowdon by the little mountain train, but if not, we set off up the ascent till, just below the steepest part, we turn off a little from the path to look at the wonderful hollow of Cwmglas, high up in the mountain-side, with its two tiny tarns, surrounded by "striated" or glacier-marked rocks.

A steep scramble brings us to the top of Snowdon, and if it is a clear day a glorious view rewards us. Beyond the line of sea is the blue range of the Wicklow Mountains in Ireland; below us, half hidden by the crags and shoulders of the huge mass, lie lakes and valleys, and the quiet lowlands stretching to the borders of the Atlantic.

Through one of the loveliest of these valleys we reach the mountain-girt village of Beddgelert. You all know the story of Llewelyn and his faithful dog, killed by his master because he thought he had eaten the child he had in reality saved from a wolf. Here you may see the stones which mark his tomb; but you will probably be told that the story is but a myth, and that the grave is really that of a Welsh chieftain named Gelert, and not of a dog at all. You may console yourselves with knowing that, whether this is true or not, the picturesque little village was a favourite hunting-spot for the Llewelyn whose story we know in history, and that the curious little church there is part of one of the oldest monasteries in Wales.

Another beautiful valley leads to the famous pass and bridge of Aberglaslyn. Here the huge cliffs on either hand approach so closely to one another that there is barely room for road and river; and the wooded slopes, as they near the water, afford a strong contrast to the wild rocks above.

After this rugged splendour, the prettiness of the Fairy Glen at Bettws-y-Coed will seem tame enough. We will not linger there, but will finish our glimpse of this land of Llewelyn by a visit to Conway Castle, built by Edward I. in 1283, to safeguard this part of Wild Wales that he had so hardly won.

The town of Conway, "rugged without, beautiful within," is a fine example of the fortified walled towns of the Middle Ages. The walls are triangular, and are said to represent a Welsh harp, and are entered by crumbling stone gateways.

Above them towers the castle of Edward I., in which he was himself besieged on one occasion by the rebel Welsh, and was only saved by the arrival of his fleet.

The poet Gray makes this neighbourhood the scene of an event upon which the light of history throws grave doubt. The English King, believing that the conquest of Wales would never be completed while the bards remained to stir up the patriotic zeal of their fellow-countrymen, is said to have ordered a general massacre of them on the banks of the River Conway. It was the prophetic curse pronounced on the King by one of these bards, standing "on a rock, whose haughty brow frowns o'er old Conway's foaming flood," which

"Scattered wild dismay As down the steep of Snowdon's shaggy side He wound with toilsome march his long array."

In spite of "Cambria's curse and Cambria's tears," the English King must have felt fairly secure within the massive walls of the castle, whose banqueting-hall, now open to the sky, and ivy-grown, is of such noble length and breadth that it might well have contained a regiment of retainers. The passionate patriotism of Wales had little chance against the solid strength of English builders and English troops.

# X
# In Glendower Land

As the name of Llewelyn is connected with the Snowdon district, so the name of another Welsh hero, Owen Glendower, lives still in that valley of the Dee that lies between Corwen and Llangollen.

The valley itself is one of the most interesting in Wales. Almost of a horseshoe shape, it is bounded by ranges of mountains, not very high, but beautiful in shape and colour. On one side, a blaze of yellow gorse, Moel Gamelin rears his rounded head; on the other the heather-clad heights of the Berwyns invite us to scramble up their slopes and to walk along the sky-line to the end of the vale. In the hollow lies the picturesque little market-town of Llangollen, and above it the steep cone-shaped hill is crowned by the ruined castle of Dinas Bran.

In the old days this castle must have been of great importance, for it guarded the entrance to the kingdom of Powys, the middle kingdom of Wales. It was the stronghold of Madoc, Lord of Powys, and of his son Griffith, who died in Llewelyn's last desperate struggle for freedom, both of whom were the ancestors of Owen Glendower himself.

Nowadays we shall find a relic of olden times in the harpist who sits upon the summit and plays Welsh airs, full of mournful sweetness, to those who visit the ruins. Below in the half-hidden Valle Crucis, lies one of the most famous of

Welsh abbeys, which we are going to explore, in order to find the resting-place of these ancestors of Glendower.

In former days Valle Crucis Abbey, founded by the Lords of Dinas Bran, was noted for its hospitality—a virtue of which we are reminded by the ruins of a large hostel, or guest-house, and by the fish-ponds which still exist. Here are the monks' dormitories; and here, in the chapel, below the beautiful remains of the east window, lie the battered tombs of Madoc, the founder, and his son. Returning to Llangollen, and passing along the Holyhead road, we presently come to Glyndyfrdwy, that "glen of the Dee" from which our hero Owen took his surname.

Like most young Welshmen of noble birth after the Conquest of Wales, Owen Glendower was brought up in England. Shakespeare makes him remind Hotspur that—

"I can speak English, lord, as well as you, For I was trained up in the English Court, Where, being but young, I framed to the harp, Many an English ditty lovely well."

When Henry IV. became King, Owen appealed to him against Lord Grey of Ruthin, who had seized a piece of his moorland. The King favoured Lord Grey, and earned the lifelong hatred of his rival, who promptly recovered his land by force of arms. Grey of Ruthin took a mean revenge. When Henry summoned his Welsh barons, among others, to aid him in a war with Scotland, he suppressed the message that summoned Glendower, and then denounced him to the King as a traitor for not obeying his call. Glendower's house was immediately besieged, and he had only just time to escape to the woods. Now, Owen was no mean and unknown Welsh knight. He was as learned in books as he was skilled in warfare, and his house at Sycherth, ten miles from his native valley, was famous for its hospitality. His wife and children were of noble breed; as a poet of the day sings: "His wife,

the best of wives, beneficent mother of a beautiful nest of chieftains. Happy am I in her wine and metheglyn."

So, after a century of peace, when this descendant of the last Llewelyn raised the standard of revolt on the banks of the Dee, the Welshmen of the districts far and wide flocked to his aid, singing with the bard, Red Iolo:

"Thy high renown shall never fail; Owen Glendower, the Great, the Good, Lord of Glyndyfrdwy's fertile vale, High born, princely Owen, hail!"

Ruthin, the stronghold of Lord Grey, now a quiet country-town, was first attacked and burnt to the ground. Before Henry's army, under the government of Harry Percy, or Hotspur, and the young Prince Henry, then a boy of fourteen, could act against them, the revolt had spread all over Wales, and had declared its aim to be independence of English rule. The success with which Glendower met soon earned for him the reputation of a wizard.

"I can call spirits from the vasty deep," Shakespeare makes him boast to Hotspur; who rudely replies: "Ay, but will they answer?" But let the rough Northern Earl scoff as he might, Owen certainly met with almost uncanny success. The English troops, "bootless and weatherbeaten," were driven back across the borders again and again. Not only North Wales, but the South country also rose under him. Midway between the two stands "Pumlumon," better known as Plynlimmon, a five-pointed peak that rises, almost solitary, from the surrounding plain. Upon this top Glendower planted his standard, and from thence he managed to capture Mortimer, the powerful English Earl of royal blood, who became before long his son-in-law.

Owen was now openly acknowledged as Prince of Wales; castle after castle fell into his hands, and Parliaments were held by him at Dolgelly, under the shadow of Cader Idris, and

elsewhere. But meantime Prince Henry, the future Henry V., was growing up and learning the art of war. It was he who, while Owen was busy in South Wales, came to his own valley of Glyndyfrdwy, and burnt his house down. For seven years the war went on, until the land was wellnigh ruined and the people weary of warfare. Pardons were freely offered and as freely accepted, until at last Owen Glendower found himself deserted. Still he would not give in, and when Henry V., soon after he was made King, sent him an unasked for pardon by the hands of Glendower's own son, it came too late; the hero of Wales' last bid for independence was dead.

Nearly eighty years later Wales recovered her name for loyalty to an English Sovereign when a certain Henry Tudor, grandson of a Welsh country gentleman who had married a King's widow, landed at Milford Haven, and, with the aid of his fellow-countrymen, won the Battle of Bosworth, and was crowned King as Henry VII. And so, when Henry VIII., his son, wished to bring about the Union of England and Wales by Act of Parliament, no voice was lifted against it. But if Henry thought by this Act, and by forbidding all magistrates in Wales to use the Welsh language, he was going to make the country actually a part of England, he was greatly mistaken. The upper classes might flock to the English Court and forget their Welsh homes, but the greater part of the people—the workers of the nation—kept their own speech, their own customs, their own traditions. The days of warfare were over; but still you can tell a Welshman from an Englishman wherever he is found. He may talk the purest English, but the fall and rise of his voice as he talks differs from the more monotonous tones of his Anglo-Saxon companion. He is more excitable, more easily moved to wrath, or tears, or laughter, and he possesses, as a rule, a far more vivid imagination than is found anywhere outside the Celtic race of which he forms a part.

# XI
# A Welsh Market-Town

We have come to the end of Glendower's story, but before we leave his part of the country altogether let us pay a visit to Corwen, the old market-town that lies so near his own valley.

Someone has said that Corwen is "relentlessly tucked away under the dark shoulder" of the heather-clad Berwyns, for above it lies the height of Pen-y-Pigyn, which certainly keeps the sun off very effectually. In the porch of the old church, indeed, we shall find a great stone, called by a Welsh name that means "the pointed stone in the icy nook." A legend, found in many other parts of Wales, says that the builders vainly tried to erect the church, which was built before the town, on a sunnier position farther down the valley, but every night the walls were destroyed and the materials carried down to the sunless spot under the hill. Just above the vestry door of that same church is a curious mark, said to have been made by the dagger of Glendower, flung by him in a fit of rage one day from the top of Pen-y-Pigyn.

So far away is Corwen from mines or flannel mills or tourist centres, that it forms in many ways a good example of a Welsh country-town, as it might have existed not long after the days of Glendower himself.

The great interest lies in the monthly fair-day, when the streets and market-place are full of shaggy Welsh ponies, black-

faced mountain-sheep, and cattle with immense horns. At every corner stand groups of farmers, talking eagerly with hands and shoulders as much as with lips, and with that curious rise and fall of the voice which, they tell us, is the secret of Welsh oratory. Of that conversation the Saxon from over the border understands not a word; but no sooner does he make a remark than with the utmost ease the Welshmen respond in excellent English. The power of expressing themselves equally well in both languages is a striking feature of even the most uneducated classes in Wales. Only here and there in some farm hidden far away among the hills could one meet with the experience of one who, weary and thirsty after a long tramp over the high moors, approached a tiny farm-house and asked the old woman who opened the door for a cup of milk. A shake of the head was the only reply. "But you must have milk or water in the house!" persisted the visitor. Another shake and a stream of words in an unknown tongue followed. Not to be baffled, the Saxon raised his hand to his mouth and made as if to drink.

With a cry of delight the old dame rushed away, and returned with a large bowlful of liquid, of which the traveller eagerly partook. It was fine thick butter-milk, but, alas! it was quite sour!

Perhaps, however, the chief regret in the visitor's mind was the impossibility of explaining why the bowl was returned full to the brim, for the old dame's puzzled look said plainly enough: "What more *could* the stranger want than good Welsh butter-milk?"

Meantime the market-women have spread out their goods—poultry, butter, eggs, and flowers—on the market-stalls in a picturesque fashion enough. Many of the women themselves are worth the attention of an artist, with their strong brown faces, black crisp hair, and very dark blue eyes, "put in with a smutty finger," as someone has well described them.

Fifty years ago you would have seen them dressed in short red skirts, buckled shoes, crossed bodices, and tall steeple-crowned hats worn over caps; but these, unfortunately, have vanished.

The men—farmers or cattle-drovers for the most part—differ in face more than they do in name. To English ears everyone seems to be called either David Mor-r-gan (with a beautiful roll to the "r") or Owen Jones. But to the careful eye the difference between the two original races is clear. The one is still short, smaller in build, and very dark-haired; the other is tall, ruddy, with long loose limbs and fiery red hair.

Borrow, whose amusing description of his walks in "Wild Wales" you will like some day to read, thus describes a fair at Llangollen some fifty years ago, and from what one knows of these country-towns, one would not expect to find things very different to-day.

"The fair," he says, "was held in and near a little square in the south-east quarter of the town. It was a little bustling fair, attended by plenty of people from the country. A dense row of carts extended from the police-station half across the space. These carts were filled with pigs, and had stout cord nettings drawn over them, to prevent the animals escaping.

"By the sides of these carts the principal business of the fair appeared to be going on—there stood the owners, male and female, higgling with Llangollen men and women who came to buy. The pigs were all small, and the price given seemed to vary from eighteen to twenty-five shillings. Those who bought pigs generally carried them away in their arms, and then there was no little diversion. Dire was the screaming of the porkers, yet the purchaser always knew how to manage his bargain, keeping the left arm round the body of the swine, and with the right hand fast gripping the ear. Some few were led away by strings.

"There were some Welsh cattle, small, of course, and the purchasers of these seemed to be Englishmen—tall, burly fellows

in general, far exceeding the Welsh in height and size....

"Now and then a big fellow made an offer, and held out his hand for a little Celtic grazier to give it a slap—a cattle bargain being concluded by a slap of the hand—but the Welshman generally turned away with a half-resentful exclamation.

"There were a few horses and ponies in a street leading into the fair—I saw none sold, however....

"Now, if I add there was much gabbling of Welsh round about, and here and there some slight sawing of English—that in the street leading from the north there were some stalls of gingerbread, and a table at which a queer-looking being, with a red Greek cap on his head, sold rhubarb, herbs, and phials containing I know not what—I think I have said all that is necessary about Llangollen Fair."

Perhaps, however, we should visit Corwen or any other Welsh market-town on a Sunday to see the most striking characteristics of the people.

The streets are nearly deserted, and a strange stillness broods over the place. At the open door of some of the cottages an aged woman sits with a Welsh Bible on her knees, and keeps an eye upon the toddling baby at her feet. Everyone else has vanished, and not until a burst of melody sounds from the plainly-built chapels which occur so frequently on the highways and within the township, is their whereabouts revealed. Such singing it is, too! It has been said that the Welsh people sing naturally in parts, and certainly it seems as though nothing but years of training would produce such a result with English choirs, not to speak of a whole congregation, as is the case in Wales. In perfect time and tune the beautiful old Welsh melodies ring forth, and we begin to realize what a large part this hymn-singing and fiery enthusiastic preaching plays in the daily life of this emotional and deeply religious people.

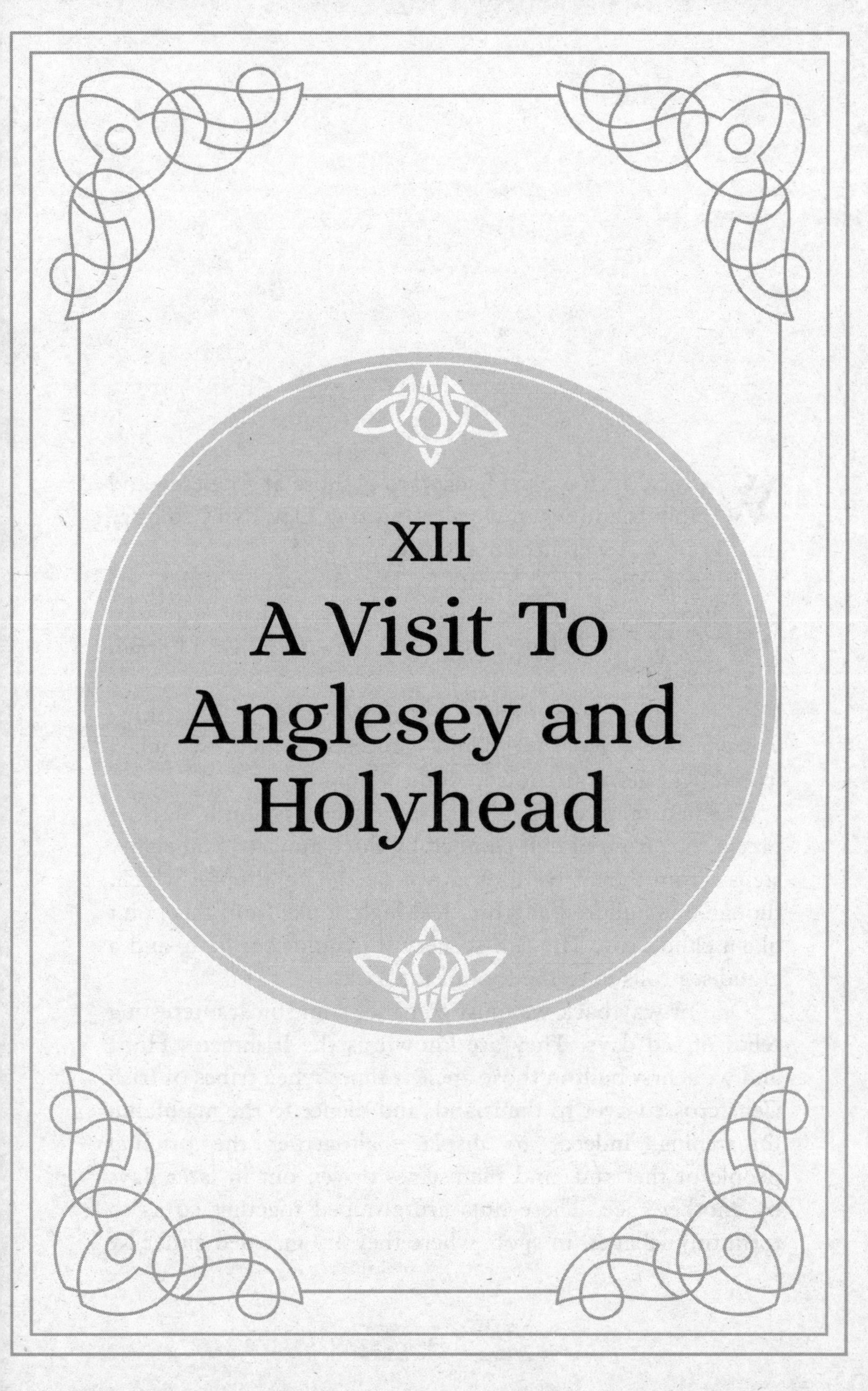

# XII
# A Visit To Anglesey and Holyhead

We took such a brief backward glimpse at Anglesey and Holy Island when we were visiting Llewelyn's country that we may as well now make a longer visit.

Crossing the Menai Straits by the suspension bridge, we pass through a treeless moorland and over a causeway into Holy Island, from whence rises up the great headland known as Holyhead.

"A divine promontory," Ruskin calls it, "looking westward—the Holy Headland—still not without awe when its red light glares first through the gloom."

The first thing we shall want to visit here is South Stack, a precipitous mass of cliff climbed by three hundred and eighty steps. From thence we look down on the lighthouse, which, though one hundred and fifty feet high, looks from this point like a child's toy. The cliff scenery is magnificent here, and a grand sea rolls in to the foot of the rocks.

On our way back we must go to see some most interesting relics of old days. They are known as the Irishmen's Huts, and were first built in those ancient times when tribes of Irish Celts crossed over to the island, and thence to the mainland, threatening, indeed, to displace altogether the original people of the land, and themselves driven out in later days by another race. These huts are grouped together so as to form tiny villages, in spots where they are guarded either by

steep rocks or by roughly-constructed walls. They are round in shape, and built of stone, though the remains of the walls are now not more than two feet high. All the entrances look towards the south, as though the inhabitants knew the value of sunshine; and the doorways are formed of two upright stones, with another placed across the top. The roofs were probably thatched or turfed over poles, which stretched from one wall to the other.

From what was found under the ground on which they stand when it was examined some years ago, it seems as though some of these huts were used for living in, some for bathing, some for working metal, some for kitchens. Necklaces of jet, stone lamps, weapons of bronze, and moulds for making bronze buttons were found in some. In others there are the remains of an apparatus for working metal; in others there are tanks, in which water was boiled by throwing hot stones into the water they contained.

Retracing our way by rail, we pass the village of Llangadwaladr, the home of the last British Prince to hold the title of King of All Britain. The son of this Prince, Cadwaladr, who lived and died in the seventh century, is buried in the church of the place that bears his name, the "enclosure, or church, of Cadwaladr." But the chief interest lies in his father, Cadwallon, and his cousin, Brian, who together won one of the last great battles in the cause of British freedom against the English conquerors.

Cadwallon, son of King Cadfan, and Edwin, son of King Ethelfrid of Northumbria, were both born about the same year in the island of Anglesey, or Mona, as the Celts call it; for the Celtic mother of Edwin had been driven out of the royal palace, and had returned to her former home. The boys were brought up together in Brittany, another Celtic kingdom, and returned together to Anglesey, where they lived until, on the

death of his father, Cadwallon was chosen King of All Britain. This was, however, but an empty title, for almost at that very time Edwin left the island and made his way to Northumbria, where he seized the kingdom and with it much of the land of the Britons which lay upon its borders. But Cadwallon cared not, because he had been his friend.

Now the heart of Brian, the nephew of the British King, was very sore because of the sufferings of his fellow-countrymen at the hands of the English conquerors. One day, as he hunted the otter with his uncle on the banks of a river, the King was overcome with heat and lay down to sleep, putting his head on the lap of the lad.

But Brian's heart was so heavy that his tears ran down upon the face of Cadwallon, who muttered uneasily: "It rains, it rains!"

Then, opening his eyes, he saw the blue sky above him, and said to his nephew: "Surely there has been a shower, and now the sun is shining. But where is the rainbow?"

And Brian said: "My lord, it shines upon the head of Edwin!"

Then Cadwallon saw his tearful face, and asked him what he meant; and Brian told him all his woe. Whereupon Cadwallon swore to devote the rest of his life to winning back the land of Britain for her own people.

But the strong King of Northumbria drove him back from his borders again and again, and almost in despair he set sail with Brian to seek help from Brittany. A great storm arose, however, drove the ship upon the rocks, and everyone was drowned save Cadwallon and his nephew, who were cast upon a desert island.

There, says the tale, King Cadwallon would have died of hunger and heart-break had not the devoted Brian secretly cut off a slice of his own flesh, which he roasted and gave to his

uncle, saying it was venison. The King ate and took courage, and after a time they were able to pass over the stormy sea in the wrecked boat to Brittany.

The King of that land promised help, but meantime Brian heard that his sister had been taken a captive to Edwin's Court, and that Edwin himself was much under the influence of a certain clever counsellor, who was especially hostile to the Britons.

So Brian, dressed in beggar's rags, but carrying a spiked staff, crossed to Wessex, and made the long journey on foot to York to the palace of Edwin. Standing outside, among a crowd of outcasts, he presently saw his sister come forth from the Queen's household with a pitcher on her head to draw water from the well. At once he pretended to ask alms of her, and meantime told her who he was, and bade her point out to him the wily counsellor among Edwin's followers. At that moment the latter came out with a bag of money for the beggars, and Brian, rushing forward, pierced him to the heart with his pointed staff, and then vanished among the crowd.

Fleeing from thence to Penda, the strong King of the Mercians, Brian won him over to his uncle's side, and forthwith Cadwallon, Brian, and Penda marched against Edwin in a great battle, in which the King of Northumbria, Cadwallon's foster-father, was defeated and slain.

Penda took care to secure the northern kingdom for himself, but until his death Cadwallon earned his title to some extent by becoming undisputed ruler over Wales, Devon, Cornwall, and the land now known as Westmorland and Cumberland.

He married a sister of grim King Penda, and their son was the peaceful Cadwaladr, in whose reign much of the land of the Britons was again lost to them. Never again did Welsh Prince claim to be King of All Britain, even in name.

[illegible] the King of the Lord [illegible] and [illegible] when they were able to [illegible]

[illegible]

[illegible]

[illegible]

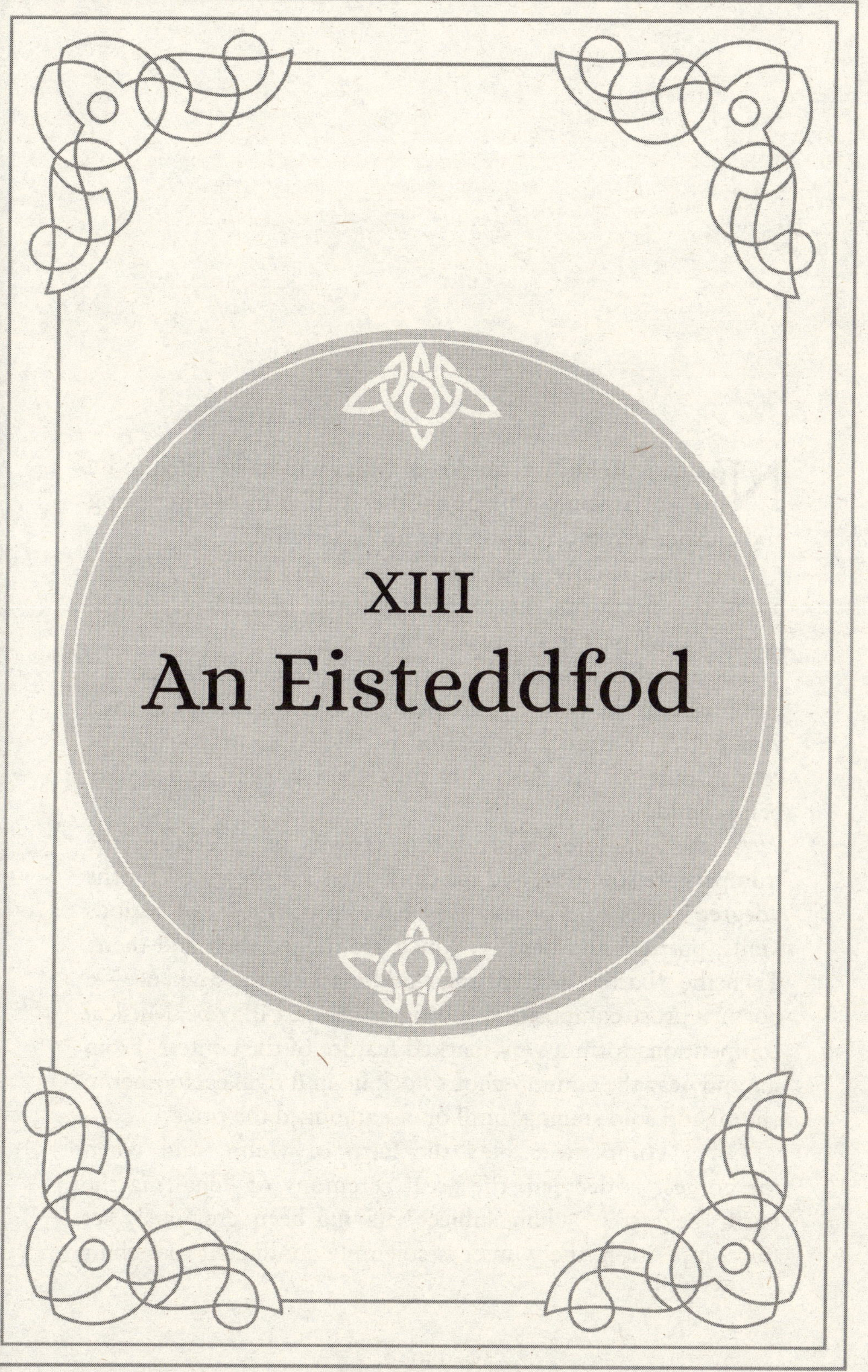

XIII

# An Eisteddfod

No one who knows and loves Wales will have failed to be present at some time or another at that most interesting and curious ceremony known as an Eisteddfod.

The name simply means a "sitting," and probably refers, not to the spectators, but to the "chairing" of the bard, which forms a chief part in the proceedings.

These gatherings, for the purpose of preserving the poetry and music of the country, are held all over the land; but each year a great national Eisteddfod is held at some convenient centre; and of this notice is published a year and a day beforehand.

At the appointed time, before crowds of spectators, the trumpets are sounded, and the candidates are presented for the "degree" of bard. For this they have to pass tests of various kinds, poetical and literary, which are judged then and there. Then the "bards" present their addresses to the audience—a poem, a prose composition, a song, as the case may be. Musical competitions form a very marked feature of the contest. From far and near the country choirs flock in, and rival each other in choral and solo singing, until one is adjudged the prize.

Other competitors play the harp or violin, and when the contest is decided, the great ceremony of "chairing the bard" begins. A "chair subject" having been previously set for competition, the winner is solemnly conducted to a chair

of carved oak, a naked sword is held over his head, and he is greeted with the blare of trumpets as the bard. A concert, given by well-known singers, closes the proceedings, which have often lasted for two or three days.

This ceremony dates from very far-off times. It may, indeed, be found in some form in the time of that wonderful King Arthur of whom you have all heard.

He, as you know, was King of Britain in the "days before history," and at his Court it was the custom to set tests of valour to his knights. Once he set seven of them to find fair Olwen, daughter of Thornogre Thistlehair, chief of the Giants, and they were given a year and a day for their quest. Of the many wonderful adventures that befell them you may read in a delightful collection of Welsh stories called *The Mabinogion*, or "Book for Girls and Boys."

At another Yule-tide his nephew, Sir Gawayne, was put to a more severe test. A Green Knight of immense stature rode into the dining-hall of the King, and dared any knight present to give him, who was armed only with a holly-stick, a blow with an axe, on the condition that he should receive a blow in return a year and a day after the event.

Sir Gawayne proved himself the only one who was not too dismayed at such a condition, and with one good blow cut off the Green Knight's head. The latter, however, merely picked it up, and held it aloft, upon which the head, opening its eyes and addressing Sir Gawayne, said:

"Look you, be ready as you have promised, and seek me till you find me. Get you to Green Chapel a year and a day from now, there to receive a blow on New Year's Eve."

The adventures of Sir Gawayne must be read elsewhere. They form the subject of a fine English poem of the fourteenth century, and were certainly of the nature of a test of courage and endurance.

By the sixth century the Eisteddfod seems to have become more of a test of poetical and musical talent than of knightly skill and prowess. Those who proved themselves worthy at the yearly gathering were classed as bards, and were given the right of entry into the castles of all Welsh barons and Princes. At one of the earliest of these meetings Gwynedd, Prince of North Wales, in order to show how superior vocal music was to that performed on instruments, offered a prize to the bards who should swim over the Conway.

Eagerly the test was accepted, but when they reached the farther bank the unfortunate harpists found their strings were ruined by the water, while the singers were merely braced up to even more successful efforts than before.

In the twelfth century we hear of a very notable Eisteddfod held at Caerwys, now a little country-town, hidden away on a high tableland among the hills, but notable in former days as the favourite residence of the last Llewelyn. It was his ancestor, Griffith, who held there a gathering, "to which there repaired all the men of Wales and also some from England and Scotland," says the proud historian of the event. And another is described as taking place at Cardigan Castle, where assembled many bards, harpers, and minstrels, "the best to be found in all Wales."

In the last century this interesting old custom, which had become much neglected, was revived, and now almost every Welsh town can boast of its own little Eisteddfod, in which the various choirs of church and chapel, the plough-boy poet and the clever school-child, all play their part in keeping alive that spirit of poetry and music which is characteristic of the national character of Wild Wales.

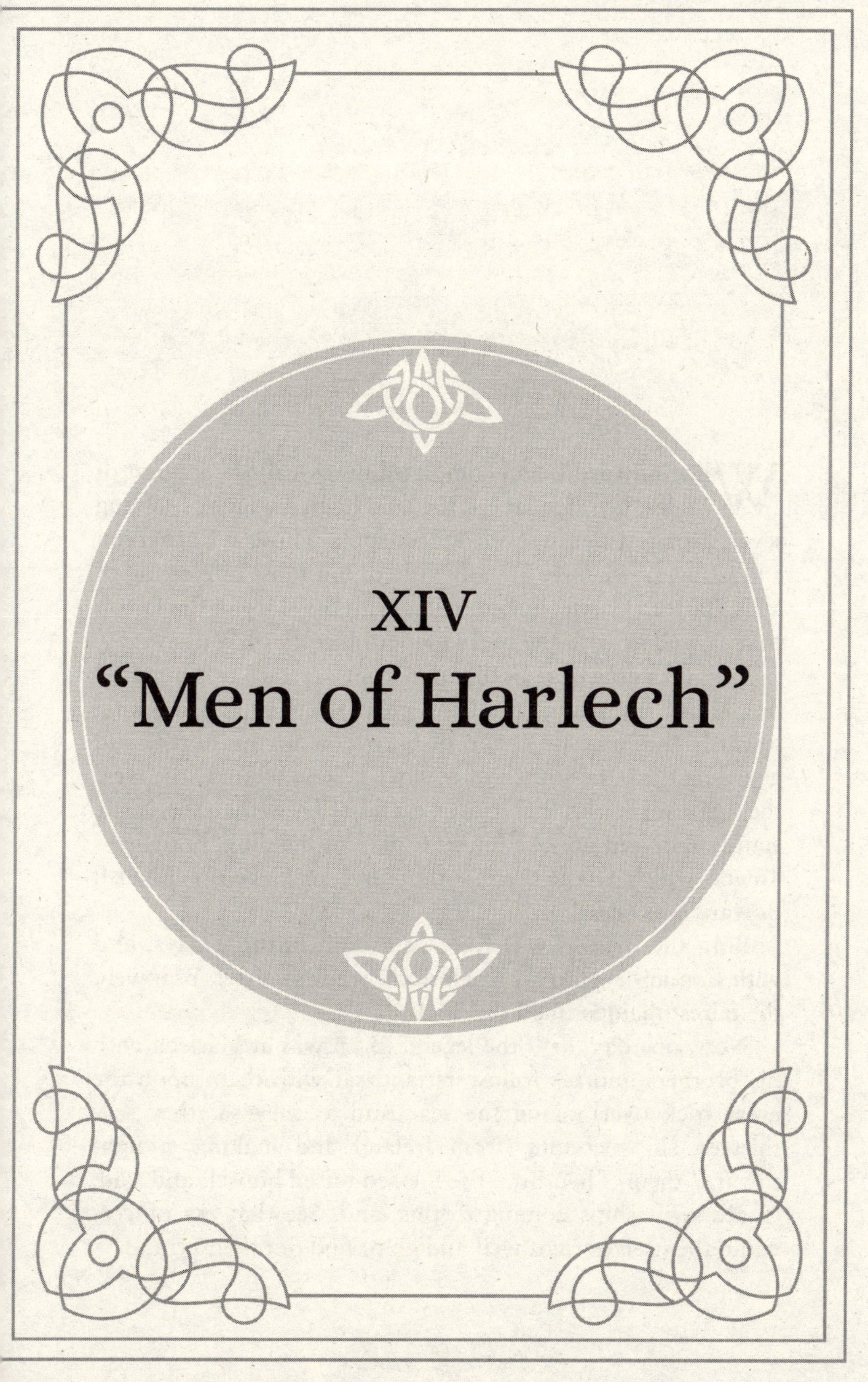

# XIV
# "Men of Harlech"

When Edward I. had completed his so-called conquest of Wales, he safeguarded the land he had won by building seven strong castles in seven danger-spots. Those at Carnarvon and Conway we have already visited, but most interesting of all is Harlech Castle, linked as it is with the story of the far-off past as well as with the more modern history of Wales.

Built on a crag of rock that juts from a terrace two hundred feet above the plain, stand the great stone towers, looking towards the majestic range of Snowdon to the north, and guarding the wide stretch of country below; while to the west they gaze over the Irish Sea. Legend tells us that the castle stands upon the site of a far more ancient building, Branwen's Tower, which stood there a thousand years before English Edward was heard of.

Bran the Blessed was King of Britain in those days, and with him in his fortress at Harlech lived his sister, Branwen, the fairest maiden in all the land.

Now, one day, says the legend, Bran was at Harlech with his brothers and his followers, and sat with them upon the great rock overlooking the sea. And as they sat they saw thirteen ships coming from Ireland and making straight towards them. Then Bran the Blessed raised himself and said: "I see swift ships coming to this land. See that my officers equip themselves right well and go to find out their errand."

So the officers did so, and when the ships drew near the shore, behold, they saw that they were very richly furnished, with ropes of silk and flags of satin. And in the foremost stood one who lifted a shield high above the bulwarks, and the point of the shield was held upward in token of peace.

Then the strangers landed, and when they had saluted the King, Bran from his rock said unto them: "Heaven prosper you, my friends. To whom do these ships belong, and who amongst you is your chief?"

And they said: "Behold, the King of Ireland, Matholwch, is here as suitor unto thee, and he will not land unless thou grant him his desire."

"And what is his desire?" asked the King.

And they said: "He would make alliance with thee, lord, by taking in marriage Branwen, thy fair sister; that, if it seem good to thee, the Island of the Mighty might be joined to the Island of the Blessed, and so both become more powerful."

"Let him land," said King Bran, "and we will take counsel together upon this matter."

So the two Kings met in friendly wise, and it was arranged that Matholwch should marry Branwen, the fairest damsel in the land, and that the wedding should take place at Aberffraw, in Anglesey.

There a great feast was held, all in tents, "for no house could contain Bran the Blessed." But when the banquet was at its height, came in the bride's half-brother, Evnyssian, and, out of spite, because he had not been consulted in the matter, he went to the stables where the horses of the Irish King had been housed, and "cut off their lips to the teeth and their ears close to their heads, and their tails close to their backs, and their eyelids to the bone."

In his wrath, when he discovered this, the Irish King would have broken off the alliance and declared war there and then,

but Bran managed to appease his anger by giving him "a silver rod as tall as himself and a plate of gold as wide as his face;" and so he sailed away to the Isle of Saints with his fair bride.

But he never forgot the insult that had been offered him, for his people, jealous of the strange Queen, were constantly reminding him of it; and after her little son, Gwern, was born, the King deposed her from her place at his side, and ordered her to be cook in his palace.

Sad indeed was Branwen, for she was lonely in the land; but she reared a starling in the cover of her kneading-trough, and when she had written down the story of her wrongs, she tied the letter under the bird's wing, and set it free. The bird, it is said, flew straight to Carnarvon, the abode at that time of King Bran, perched upon his shoulder, and flapped his wings till the letter was seen and taken from him.

Full of anger at the treatment his sister had received, King Bran called together his fighting-men and embarked for Ireland. But Matholwch had no will for warfare, and, having held converse with him, offered to make up for the wrongs offered to his wife by giving up his crown at once to his young son Gwern. To this Bran agreed, and forthwith the Irish King ordered a great banquet to be prepared, that the contract might be sealed.

Now, the boy Gwern was present at this banquet, and showed himself so lovable and so fair that all admired him. But his wicked uncle, Evnyssian, who had already wrought so much evil, waited till he came near, and then of a sudden seized him by neck and ankles, and threw him into the great fire that blazed upon the hearth. In vain did Branwen try to fling herself into the flames that she might save her son. The deed was done before she could grasp him, and his fair body had become a heap of ashes. Because of this foul deed did bitter warfare break out between the two countries, and

so hard went the fighting against the British that at length only seven knights were left alive on the side of Bran, and he himself was sorely wounded in the head, so that he was about to die.

Then Bran the Blessed commanded this poor remnant of his followers to strike off his head and bear it to his native land, and he bade them keep it at Harlech for seven years, and then to set it upon the White Mount in the city of Lud; which place is now called Tower Hill in London town.

So the seven knights returned to Harlech with the head of their King, and with them they brought his sister, the unhappy Branwen. And on their way they rested in Anglesey, where Branwen, looking first towards Ireland and then towards Britain, cried with tears: "Woe is me that I was ever born, for two islands have been destroyed because of me!"

Then died poor Branwen of a broken heart, and they buried her in Anglesey, at a spot known henceforth as Ynys Branwen, "where a square grave was made for her on the banks of the Alaw, and there was she laid."[1]

Early in the last century a four-sided hole was discovered by a farmer in this place, covered over with coarse flagstones. Within was an urn, placed with its mouth downwards, and full of ashes and fragments of bone. The urn was certainly one of that period known as the Bronze Age, and belonged to the "days before history," so we may not unsafely conclude that the ashes it contained were really those of the unhappy Branwen, sister of Bran the Blessed.

And so we come back to Harlech Castle, still with its Branwen Tower, built by Edward I. as a bulwark against the "rebel Welsh."

---

1 From *The Mabinogion*, according to the version in Rev. S. Baring-Gould's *Book of North Wales*.

In later days Owen Glendower besieged and obtained possession of the castle, and was in his turn besieged there by Prince Henry. There it was that his son-in-law, Mortimer, died, and there the wife and children of the latter took, for the last time, refuge when the place was once again captured by the English.

The Wars of the Roses caused stirring times at Harlech. The castle was held against Edward IV. by David ap Sinion, who had offered to receive there under his protection Margaret, the unfortunate widow of Henry VI., and her son, young Edward, after she had lost the Battle of Northampton.

Against this "rebel" marched Lord Herbert, who called upon David to surrender. But David had done good work for the Lancastrian cause abroad, and he now replied that "he had held a castle so long in France that all the old women in Wales had talked about it; and now he was going to hold Harlech so long that he would set the tongues of all the old women in France wagging."

Great was the slaughter in that siege, during which, it is said, the "March of the Men of Harlech" was written to stir the neighbouring vassal chieftains to revolt against the usurping Edward.

"Fierce the beacon light is flaming, With its tongues of fire proclaiming 'Chieftains, sundered to your shaming, Strongly now unite!' At the cry all Arfon rallies, War-cries rend her hills and valleys, Troop on troop, with headlong sallies, Hurtle to the fight.

"Chiefs lie dead and wounded, Yet where first 'twas grounded, Freedom's flag still holds the crag, Her trumpet still is sounded; O, there we'll keep her banner flying; While the pale lips of the dying Echo to our shout defying, 'Harlech for the right!'"

Even in the English words the chant is inspiring in the extreme; the Welsh words, joined to the warlike tune, would stir the veriest coward to play his part like a hero.

Sad to say, the brave David was forced at length to surrender, on condition that his life was granted.

To the honour of Lord Herbert be it told that when Edward wished to put David to death he sought him out, and demanded of him one of two things: either he must send David back to his castle and despatch another officer to besiege it, or he must take the life of Herbert himself in place of that of the prisoner. Finally, the King forgave David, and Harlech, the last to hold out for the Lancastrian cause, submitted.

# XV
# The Sacred River

In our peeps at North Wales we have more than once had a glimpse of the River Dee. To-day we will pretend we have taken a "coracle," one of the curious oval boats which were used in the very earliest days, and which you may sometimes see a man carrying on his shoulders from one bend of the river to another. "Carry thou me, and I will carry thee," an old Welsh proverb makes the coracle say to the fisherman; and it shall now carry us down the course of the river as far as it lies within the land of Wales. The River Dee, one of the most lovely in Wales, has always been connected with the mysterious religion of the Druids. Its very name in old days, _Deva_, meant the goddess, or the "divine one"; and its modern Welsh form, _Dwy_, means the same thing. A legend of Druid times says that the Dee springs from two fountains high up in the mountains above Bala, called Dwy Fawr and Dwy Fach, or the Great and Little Dee, whose waters pass through those of the Lake of Bala without mingling with them, and come out at its northern extremity. These fountains had their names from two individuals, Dwy Fawr and Dwy Fach, who escaped from the Deluge when all the rest of the human race were drowned, and the passing of the waters of the two fountains through the lake without mingling with its flood is an emblem of the salvation of the two individuals from the Deluge, of which the lake is a type.

Probably the river was worshipped as a goddess in those days, and when Wales learnt the Christian faith, it would be but fitting that her bank should be crowded with those who sought baptism in her waters. Nowadays, too, it is no uncommon sight to see a little group of people by the waterside presiding over the baptism of one or more of their companions.

Soon after leaving the lake the Dee passes through a district that is closely connected with the youth of that great Celtic hero, King Arthur. There are few parts of Wales which—by their names, at least—allow us to forget that Arthur and his Court played a famous part in Britain in the days before history. And here we have Caer Gai, the ancient stronghold of Sir Kay, the foster-brother of Arthur, who could make himself as tall as the tallest tree in the forest, or lie hidden in lake or river for nine days and nights, if needs be. Such fire was in his nature that when they needed warmth his companions had but to kindle the piled wood at his finger; he could walk through torrents of rain as dry as on a summer's day; he could go for nine days and nights without sleep; and no doctor could heal the wounds made by his sword.

It was in this district of Penllyn, opposite to the hill of Yr Aran, which he calls "Rauran," that Spenser in his great poem makes King Arthur describe the way his boyhood was passed in the "stronghold of Kay," or Caer Gai:

"Whose dwelling is low in a valley green Under the fort of Rauran, mossy hoar, From whence the River Dee, as silver clean, His tumbling billows rolls with gentle roar; There all my days he trained me up in virtuous lore."

But, apart from legend, Caer Gai touches history itself. From its well-preserved ramparts and "fosse," or moat, enclosing what is now a farm-house, we see that it must have once been a Roman fortress. Roman urns have been dug up

here, and not very many years ago a ploughman turned up a stone with an inscription that showed it must have been placed there by Roman soldiers about A.D. 105.

Leaving Llyn Tegid, or Bala Lake, behind us, we set off down our river to Corwen and Llangollen. These places we have already visited, so we will only stay to notice the lovely scenery of this part of the Dee, so dear to fishers. Not far from where the river bends north-east to Chester and the sea, stands Chirk Castle, and near by, in order to reach it from Llangollen, we shall pass the line of Offa's Dyke, a bank with a moat below it that ran from the mouth of the Dee to the mouth of the Wye, which was erected by a King of Mercia in the eighth century as a barrier beyond which no Welshman might pass.

For the rest of its course, therefore, the Dee really forms part of the boundary-line between England and Wales, and though we shall be sorely tempted to linger when we come to the beautiful old city of Chester, gazing down from its ancient walls upon the broad river below, we must remind ourselves that this is English soil, and leave the sacred waters of the Dee to empty themselves by a very long estuary into the sea some miles below Flint Castle, the last refuge of the unhappy Richard II. before he gave himself into the hands of Bolingbroke.

# XVI
# A Peep at Pembroke

To-day we will leave North Wales and travel south to take a glimpse at Pembrokeshire, in some ways one of the most interesting counties in Wales.

Between the northern and southern parts of the country runs a stream, flowing into St. Bride's Bay, which divides the Welsh Pembroke from a district known as "Little England beyond Wales."

Here, in this latter region, one hears nothing but English spoken. The towns, the people, are typically English, or, at least, very far from being typically Welsh. This is how a seventeenth-century writer accounts for the fact:

"This same division was in ancient time inhabited wholly by Welshmen, but a great part thereof was won from them by the Englishmen under the conduct of Earl Strongbow, and divers others, and the same planted with Englishmen whose posterity enjoys it to this day, and keep their language among themselves without receiving the Welsh speech or learning any part thereof, and hold themselves so close to the same as to this day they wonder at a Welshman coming among them, the one neighbour saying to the other: 'Look! there goeth a Welshman!'"

The interesting thing about this is that these people of South Pembroke were probably not English at all in origin, but Flemings, who came over from Flanders many centuries

ago, and settled there with their woollen manufactures—a trade which perhaps accounts for the superiority of "Welsh flannel" to-day.

These were, like their Welsh neighbours, a very religious and emotional people, and more ready, perhaps, than the former to leave the land of their adoption for the perils of the Holy War. For a writer of the time of the early Crusades tells the story of a certain Archbishop's journey through Wales to rouse volunteers for the war in far-off Palestine; and to him "it appears wonderful and miraculous that, although he addressed the Pembroke people both in the Latin and French tongues, these persons, who understood neither of these languages, were much affected, and flocked in great numbers to the cross.... They are," he goes on to say, "a brave and robust people, ever most hostile to the Welsh—a people well versed in commerce and woollen manufactures, anxious to seek gain by sea or land, in defiance of fatigue and danger, a hardy race, equally fitted for the plough or the sword."

Suppose we take a steamer from the charming little seaport town of Tenby, and follow the coast-line of Pembroke up to Milford Haven. Romantic cliffs guard the land, and limestone caverns hint at smuggling expeditions in the good old days. Here is Caldy Island, where stood one of the oldest of Benedictine priories; and here, at St. Gowan's Head, the cliff, rising to a great height above the sea, is split up into a narrow cleft by the force of the waves.

Across this chasm is built a little cell, known as St. Gowan's Chapel, from which a doorway leads to a cave in the cliff, shaped exactly like a human figure. The legend says that St. Gowan, a holy man of God, was praying in his cell when his heathen foes came battering at the door. He called upon the rock to be his shelter, and immediately it opened to admit him. When his enemies had gone away baffled, and the saint

had emerged, the impression of his form was found in the cliff; and nowadays they say that if you stand in the cavity and wish, and then turn round without changing your mind, the wish is sure to come true.

Now we are entering Milford Haven, "the finest harbour in the United Kingdom," stretching ten miles inland, with its many bays, creeks, and roadsteads. Sailing up the right-hand shore, we presently reach Pembroke Dock, two miles from the town of Pembroke, where stand the ruins of one of the earliest built and strongest of the many castles of Wales.

From its huge towers and turrets Strongbow started on that adventurous journey of his with the aim of conquering Ireland. For many years after the conquest of Wales its grim keep, with its conical roof capped by an enormous millstone, menaced the rebel Welsh. There, in 1456, was born Henry Tudor, one day to be Henry VII. of England, and there he spent the first ten years of his boyhood. There also was his landing-place when he came to drive the usurping Richard from the throne.

Its story during the Civil War is strange enough. Pembroke Castle, under Poyer, the Mayor of Pembroke, was the only place in Wales that declared for the Parliament. But it looked as though this was only done for love of opposition to the majority, for when the war was over and troops were being sent back home, Poyer refused to give up his post as Governor of the Castle, and roused up the whole of South Wales for the Royalist cause, then practically dead. Great must have been the surprise of the Puritans, but before long Cromwell himself was putting the rebels to flight and battering at the walls of Pembroke Castle, where so many had taken refuge.

"A very desperate enemy, very many of them gentlemen of quality, and thoroughly resolved," so Oliver described them. But the well of drinking-water had been captured by him, and

hunger and thirst compelled them to surrender. Poyer and two other leaders were sent to the Tower and condemned to death, but pardon being granted to two of the three, lots were then drawn. "Life given by God" was written on two slips; the third was a blank. Poyer drew the last, and, facing death with the utmost courage, was shot at Covent Garden.

It is tempting to take a glimpse at the stately ruins of Carew Castle, another great stronghold of old times; but we must hasten on to the head of the estuary, and thence by land to the ancient town of Haverfordwest, now a flourishing market-town, the most important in the county. Again the most striking feature is the great square-walled castle, concerning which the old Welsh historian tells an exciting adventure.

It so happened that a certain robber-chief was imprisoned in the dungeon of the castle at the time that the three young sons of the Earl of Pembroke and two children of the Governor were playing together within the walls. The game was shooting with bow and arrows, but the latter were so badly made that the youngsters began to lament that no one could make them well enough. Either through a chink in the wall, or by means of his gaoler, the prisoner conveyed the information that he was noted for the work of arrow-making, and the boys were soon his devoted admirers. One day the too confiding gaoler went off to his dinner, leaving the dungeon door with the key in the lock, that the boys might visit the interesting maker of arrows. No sooner were some of them inside, however, than the brigand locked them in with him, and threatened those who tried to break down the door that he would kill the children and himself unless the Governor swore to let him go free. This was done at length, in sheer despair, and the robber was allowed to depart to his lair in safety.

Haverfordwest is the nearest station to St. David's, the most famous cathedral in Wales, once the aim of many a

pilgrimage, since "two journeys to St. David's shrine counted as one to Rome." And well it might, since even now there are "sixteen miles and seventeen hills" to traverse before we reach the sacred spot.

St. David's Cathedral stands remote in a somewhat desolate country, upon a strip of craggy seaboard, "the loneliest of British fanes." "We descend a narrow street paved with rough stones, we look through a little gateway on the right, and stand astonished and delighted. A wonderful prospect bursts upon us: we behold the whole cathedral rising before us in its stern majesty, with the ruins of St. Mary's College to the right, and the magnificent remains of the Bishop's palace to the left, while the dark rocks of Carn Llidi form the background to the striking picture."[2]

The loveliness of the building itself, its massive pillars and delicate tracery, with the grey, purple, and red colours of the sandstone from which they are formed, make it one of the most beautiful of cathedrals; but the most thrilling memory in connection with it is that, when most of England was still plunged in heathen darkness, a cathedral stood in this place as the Church of West Britain and the seat of an Archbishop of the Celtic Church.

The shrine of St. David, or Dewi, the Water-drinker, the patron saint of Wales, is within, and with him lies the honour of transferring the seat of the Archbishopric from its more ancient site at Caerleon in Monmouthshire to this spot. St. David, said by one legend to have been uncle to King Arthur, became famous by a miracle that occurred in the sixth century, when he addressed a great meeting of the Fathers of the early Christian Church, and laid low the false doctrines of one Pelagius, or Morgan, who was leading the Christians of Britain and other lands astray.

2 D. T. Evans, *Welsh Pictures*.

As the saint, then Abbot of St. Patrick's Monastery, where now stands the present cathedral, addressed a crowd composed of "the saints of Anjou, the saints of England, and of the North, of Man and Anglesey, of Ireland and Devonshire and Kent," and of many other places, a white dove descended from heaven upon his shoulder. "Upon which the ground on which he was standing," says the legend, "gradually rose under him, till it became a hill, from which his voice, like a loud-sounding trumpet, was clearly heard and understood by all, both near and far off, seven thousand people, on the top of which hill a church was afterwards built, and stands till this day."

This happened farther north at Llandewi-brefi, but it was this miracle that placed the see of the Archbishopric to which St. David was at once raised, in Menevia, as this lonely district was called, instead of at Caerleon, thus fulfilling the prophecy of Merlin: "Menevia shall put on the pall of Caerleon."

# XVII
# The Devil's Bridge

Central Wales is a land of hills and breezy uplands, enclosed by low mountain-ranges full of romantic gorges and hidden valleys.

It includes the north of Cardiganshire and part of the shire of Montgomery, and is famous in history as the battle-ground upon which many a struggle between the Men of the South and the Men of the North was fought out.

The first place of interest on its coast-line is Aberystwith. Here you will find the moated mound, which is all that is left of a castle, built by Gilbert de Clare, one of the barons of Henry I., to guard his newly acquired province of Cardigan or Ceredigion; the southern part being guarded by the castle we have already seen at Cardigan itself, on the mouth of the Teify.

The much more important ruins of a castle that stand near the College, and overlook the sea, are the remains of a later building in the days of Edward I.

Close by, the fine grey building of the University College brings us back to the present day, and reminds one of the fashion in which Wales, so long supposed to be behind-hand in the march of progress, led the way by founding her own University, with noble colleges at Bangor, Aberystwith, and Cardiff, where her sons and daughters might complete the education begun in the intermediate and primary schools throughout the Principality. Not only may Wales pride herself

on her University, but also on her boldness in first making the experiment of teaching boys and girls, young men and women together on precisely equal terms—an experiment in co-education which England herself has hesitated to make.

There are many interesting expeditions to be made round this pretty seaside town. Near by is Llanbadarn, the Church of St. Paternus, a Breton monk, who, in the sixth century, brought the Christian faith to this region. This church developed into a monastery in later days, and became a refuge in the twelfth century for an unusually studious Bishop of those days, who was driven from St. David's by the rough Norman barons and their favourite priests, and who found at Llanbadarn leisure and peace to write his record of the Welsh saints in older times, and to keep a valuable "chronicle," or history, of his own day.

Along the coast is Borth, and on the beach there, "between the Dovey and Aberystwith," may have been that Weir of Gwyddno, of which we read in the first chapter. There, you will remember, the unfortunate youth Elphin found a leathern bag with a child inside, who told him that he would be to him "in the days of his distress better than any three hundred salmon." And you shall hear now how, on one occasion alone, Taliesin, the child-bard, was as good as his word.

Elphin had been made prisoner by the cruel King Maelgwn, who cast him into a dungeon, barred by thirteen locked doors. After some attempts had been made in vain to win his freedom, Taliesin bade Elphin wager the King that he had a horse both better and swifter than the King's horses. The King accepted the challenge, promised him his freedom if he should win the race, and fixed day, and time, and place for the trial of the steeds.

When all was ready, the King went thither with all his Court and four and twenty of his swiftest horses; while Elphin could only muster a sorry nag ridden by a barefoot boy.

The course was marked out and the horses placed ready, when Taliesin came running with twenty-four sprigs of holly, burnt black, in his hand, and he bade the barefoot boy place the twigs in his belt. Then, as he did so, he whispered and bade him let all the King's horses get before him, and as each overtook him, to strike the horse with a holly-twig over the crupper, and then let that twig fall, and then to take another twig and do the same to every one of the horses as he was overtaken by each.

He also told the boy to watch carefully when his own horse should stumble, and to throw down his cap on the spot.

All this was done, and every one of the King's horses, when he was struck by the holly-twig, began to lag behind, so that the horse of Elphin, ridden by the barelegged boy, won the race with ease.

So the King was forced to release Elphin, and when this was done, Taliesin took his master to the spot where his horse had stumbled, and bade workmen dig a hole there, and when they had dug deep enough they found a cauldron full of gold. Then said Taliesin:

"Elphin, take thou this as a reward for having taken me out of the weir, and reared me from that time until now." So Elphin went home a rich man to his father.

Borth is not the only place in the neighbourhood which is connected with this wonderful bard of the sixth century. His grave is said to lie among the hills above the village of Taliesin, and anyone who lies in that hollow for a night alone is said to awake next morning either a poet or a madman.

Exactly the same thing is said of the man who is bold enough to spend the night on the top of Cader Idris, the home of a giant bard who is said to have invented the harp, and which is also known to us as the second highest mountain in Wales.

If we want to take a long excursion from Aberystwith, we can visit the famous Devil's Bridge in the Plynlimmon district, which is called one of the wonders of Wales. This, of course, was visited by the indefatigable Borrow, who thus describes the spot:

"To the north, and just below the hospice, is a profound hollow, with all the appearance of the crater of an extinct volcano. At the bottom of this hollow the waters of two rivers unite—those of the Rheidol from the north, and those of the Afon-y-Mynach, or 'Monk's River,' from the south-east.

"The Rheidol, falling over a rocky precipice at the northern side of the hollow, forms a cataract very pleasant to look upon from the window of the inn. Those of the Mynach, or Rhyddfant, which pass under the celebrated Devil's Bridge, are not visible, though they generally make themselves heard. The waters of both, after uniting, flow away through a romantic glen towards the west. The sides of the hollow are beautifully clad with wood.

"Penetrate now into the hollow. You descend by successive flights of steps, some of which are very slippery and insecure. On your right is the Monk's River, roaring down its dingle in five successive falls, to join its brother, the Rheidol. Each of the falls has its own peculiar basin, one or two of which are said to be of awful depth. The length which these falls, with their basins, occupy is about five hundred feet.

"On the side of the basin of the last but one is the cave, or the site of the cave, said to have been occupied in old times by the Wicked Children, two brothers and a sister, robbers and murderers. At present it is nearly open on every side, having, it is said, been destroyed to prevent its being the haunt of other evil people....

"Of all the falls, the fifth or last is the finest. You view it from a kind of den, to which the last flight of steps, the

ruggedest and most dangerous of all, has brought you. Your position here is a wild one. The fall, which is split in two, is thundering beside you; foam, foam, foam is flying all about you; the basin or cauldron is boiling frightfully below you; grim rocks are frowning terribly above you, and above them forest trees, dank and wet with spray and mist, are distilling drops in showers from their boughs.

"But where is the bridge—the celebrated Bridge of the Evil One?

"From the bottom of the first flight of steps leading down into the hollow you see a modern-looking bridge bestriding a deep chasm or cleft to the south-east, near the top of the dingle of the Monk's River. That, however, is not the Devil's Bridge, but about twenty feet below that bridge, and completely overhung by it, don't you see a shadowy, spectral object, something like a bow, which likewise bestrides the chasm? You do? Well, that shadowy, spectral object is the celebrated Devil's Bridge. It is now quite inaccessible except to birds and the climbing, wicked boys of the neighbourhood....

"To view it properly and the wonders connected with it you must pass over the bridge above it and descend a dingle till you come to a small platform on a crag. Below you now is a frightful cavity, at the bottom of which the waters of the Monk's River, which comes tumbling from a glen to the east, whirl, boil, and hiss in a horrid pot or cauldron in a manner truly tremendous.

"On your right is a slit, through which the waters, after whirling in the cauldron, escape. The slit is wonderfully narrow, considering its height, which is considerably over a hundred feet. Nearly above you, crossing the slit, which is partially wrapped in darkness, is the far-famed bridge, the Bridge of the Evil One—a work which, though crumbling and darkly grey, does much honour to the hand that built it,

whether it was the hand of Satan or of a monkish architect, for the arch is chaste and beautiful, far superior in every respect to the one above it.

"Gaze on these objects—the horrid seething pot or cauldron, the gloomy slit, and the spectral, shadowy Devil's Bridge for about three minutes, allowing a minute to each, then scramble up the bank, for you have seen enough.

"And if pleasant recollections do not haunt you through life of the noble falls and the beautiful wooded dingles to the west of the Bridge of the Evil One, and awful and mysterious ones of the monk's boiling cauldron, the long, savage, shadowy cleft, and the grey, crumbling spectral bridge, I say boldly that you must be a very unpoetical person indeed!"[3]

---

3 Borrow, *Wild Wales*.

# XVIII
# The Glowing Mountain

Our last peep shall be taken in the busy region of South Glamorgan, where the hills and valleys present a very different scene from those amongst which we have lately wandered. For here is the home of coal—that powerful material which produces the force required for most of the machinery of the world.

Above the vales of Dowlais, Neath, and Taff, over the Rhondda Valley and the towns of Merthyr Tydvil and Aberdare, hangs a perpetual smoke-cloud from the vast furnaces which are always busy smelting iron and steel from the neighbouring coal-fields, or, west of Swansea, copper imported from abroad. Some of these valleys are simply a succession of mining villages, the home of strenuous toilers who all day and all night are working their turns, or "shifts," some underground in the mines, some at the furnaces, some sending off the coal, and iron, and copper to the great port of Cardiff, or the lesser ones at Swansea or Barry.

There is nothing very picturesque about this region, although it can boast of the ruins of many strong castles, some interesting churches, and the beautiful Vale of Glamorgan—a region of meadows and grassy slopes, upon which feed fat cows and oxen to their hearts' content.

But this is, perhaps, too tame to be attractive; nor, apart from the almost terrible interest attached to all coal-mines, is there anything to keep us lingering in the blackened valleys of the district.

There is one curious feature, however, at which you will like to take a peep. Borrow, of course, found it out, and called it the Glowing Mountain.

He was on his way to Merthyr Tydvil when, as it began to grow dark, he came to the beginning of a vast moor. In the distance he could see weird blazes and hear "horrid sounds"; and, as he went on up hills and down dales, night set in, very black and still. Having toiled to the top of a steep ascent, he stopped to take breath, and saw a glow on all sides in the heavens except in the north-east quarter.

"Turning round a corner at the top of the hill, I saw blazes here and there, and what appeared to be a Glowing Mountain in the south-east. I went towards it down a descent, which continued for a long, long way. So great was the light cast by the blazes and that wonderfully glowing object, that I could distinctly see the little stones upon the road.

"After walking for about half an hour, always going downwards, I saw a house on my left hand, and heard a noise of water opposite to it. I went to the waterfall, drank greedily, and then hurried on, more and more blazes and the glowing object looking more terrible than ever.

"It was now above me at some distance to the left, and I could see that it was an immense quantity of heated matter, like lava, occupying the upper and middle parts of a hill, and descending here and there almost to the bottom in a zigzag and winding manner. Between me and the Glowing Mountain lay a deep ravine. After a time I came to a house, against the door of which a man was leaning.

"'What is all that burning stuff above, my friend?'

"'Dross from the iron forges, sir.'"

"I now perceived a valley below me, full of lights, and, descending, reached houses and a tramway. I had blazes now all around me … and finally found myself before the Castle Inn at Merthyr Tydvil."

In the morning he revisits the scene.

"The mountain of dross which had startled me on the preceding night with its terrific glare, looked now nothing more than an immense dark heap of cinders. It is only when the shades of night have settled down that the fire within manifests itself, making the hill appear an immense glowing mass."

And so, with Borrow, we will turn our backs on the great Welsh coal-field, and say good-bye for the present to Wild Wales.